The Book of
Moons

K.M. Herbert

Fisher King Publishing

Published by

Fisher King Publishing
The Studio
Arthington Lane
Pool in Wharfedale
LS21 1JZ
England

www.fisherkingpublishing.co.uk

Cover based on photo by luizclas at pexels.com

To Nicholas, whose love and
support helped write this book.

"We are the rag and bone. We are the summer walkers of the long acre of widow Breen. We are the men of the rag and bone and we've come to pick the potato eyes out of the quality folk. We are knights of the road."

Irish Tinkers by Janine Wiedel

Chapter One
The Road to Dublin

They planned it on the way back from school.

When the rest of the girls were in the dining hall, Kathy and Sinead were packing a bag. Kathy, lying on her bed, was watching Sinead in the dimly lit room, with her auburn hair splayed out on the pillow. They listened closely for snoring and heavy breathing from the other beds. Kathy opened her mouth to speak but Sinead raised a finger to her full lips. She felt her heart beat against her chest and the weight of their packed bag on her stomach. Kathy's hand instinctively went to the cross around her neck. She thought of the few things she had in the rucksack: the only other clothing she owned, a black dress and jacket and an old paperback book given to her by her mother before she died. Kathy clung to the bag tightly and thought of Sinead's favourite wool jumper she had packed along with an extra pair of socks. They both knew it wasn't much but it was all they needed to hitchhike to Dublin.

"Let's go," Sinead whispered, pulling the thin duvet off her clothed body. Kathy did the same and slipped the rucksack onto her back. They picked up their shoes; a key part of their plan to escape without notice. Ennis Orphanage was an old building. Its damp, stone walls reverberated their footsteps when they walked its corridors.

Kathy glanced down the row of small beds with their occupants fast asleep, dreaming of their own escape. She felt a pang in her stomach. Kathy had always dreamt of running away. She had imagined this scenario over a thousand times but the feeling of freedom she had pictured felt so much lighter than this.

"We need to go," Sinead whispered as she opened the wooden door carefully so it wouldn't creak. Kathy nodded in agreement and looked behind her at the room. It wasn't safe but it was familiar. And neither Kathy nor Sinead knew what lay ahead of them in Dublin. Kathy walked into the corridor on the other side of the door.

Kathy rushed after Sinead, down the cement steps that spiralled to the ground floor. They walked past the stone angel that stared down at them each morning as they went for their breakfast. As they ran past it a shadow crossed its face. Kathy could have sworn it winked.

"Do you have the key?" Sinead asked, hurriedly.

Kathy nodded and pulled an old, black iron key from her bra. She shoved it into the lock and with one turn the front door opened with a creaking sound that caused the girls to stop and look on either side of the corridor. They heard footsteps on the stairs.

Kathy groaned. "They know we've left."

"Come on."

They ran out of the building and to the end of the garden, where a large gate loomed in front of them. Kathy's heart sunk when she spotted the padlock chained across it.

"It's locked!"

"Let's head to the chapel," Sinead urged. The shadows that chased them were catching up. The girls quickly ran along the outer fence to the back garden.

"C'mon Kath, we're almost there." Sinead reached out and grabbed Kathy's hand tightly. They ran past the plants and shrubs they walked by every Sunday morning on their way to the chapel. Its sharp iron steeple emerged from the treetops. The girls looked back and ignored the sound of shouting and cursing that trailed behind them. The chapel was surrounded by a thick hedge that separated the street from its holy walls.

"Quick Kath, through here!" Sinead pulled back the overgrowth to reveal a hole through the hedge. Kathy crawled through the branches and onto Cooks Lane.

"Give me your hand," Kathy said, as she reached for the cool grasp of her friend's arm, helping her through the earthy passage. A dull creak filled the night as the main gate opened. Kathy looked ahead at the two roads they could take.

"Let's split up," Sinead said.

The footsteps were just around the corner. Kathy spun around and looked over at Sinead with pleading eyes.

"We'll meet at the friary and find a ride from there," Sinead whispered.

"Sinead," Kathy replied, tears stinging her eyes. She reached out to grab her best friend's hand.

"It's okay, Kath. You know what to do if we don't find each other."

"I don't want to travel to Dublin without you."

"See you at the friary," Sinead replied before running past Kathy. Kathy watched the curls disappear into the fog. The voices were getting louder and the footsteps were pounding the pavement harder.

Kathy squinted down the street, trying to see where Sinead ran to but the fog was thick and the road was winding. She took a deep breath and let her legs carry her forward. At the end of the lane, she found a dark bridleway that led to a residential street. She entered it quickly. It was summer but the sky was covered with thick purple clouds. It could have easily been mistaken for dawn or dusk and the bright orb trying to protrude from the clouds could have been either the moon or the sun.

At the bottom of the bridleway, the silhouette of the friary appeared. The road ahead was empty, except for a few cars parked next to the kerb. She ran to the old ruins and as she approached, she heard voices. When Kathy reached the derelict building, she was surprised to find a crowd of people gathered around it. A fiddle was being played somewhere nearby. The people around her were laughing and cupping steaming mugs in their hands. Kathy smelled fresh bread and strong coffee. Through a set of pillars, she could make out the shapes of caravans and wagons scattered around the plot.

Kathy waited nervously. It would be past midnight now, over an hour since they had escaped the orphanage. If Sinead had taken the road to their school, she would have reached the friary by now. She felt a light breeze under her blouse. It was an unusually cool evening for August. Kathy crossed her arms around her body.

As people began to leave, Kathy's mind started to wander. Did they catch up to Sinead? Her friend was clever and would have found a place to hide. There was a petrol station, perhaps she hid behind it and waited for the nuns to walk by? She might have waited until she knew they were gone before walking to the friary. Kathy squinted at each face as the patrons passed her. She was about to turn back onto the street but a flash of red appeared in her peripheral vision. Kathy pushed through a group of laughing school girls to where she saw the red curls.

"Sinead?" she called.

Kathy listened past the people around her. She thought she heard a small voice call her name from within the friary grounds. Kathy ran into the area where the caravans were arranged into a spiral. She wrapped her arms across her blouse and walked through the Franciscan arches that led to the centre of their camp. The gypsies, in their coloured garments, were removing the ribbons and flags they had tied between their caravans. Others were extinguishing the candles which had been set along the walls of the friary. Most of the patrons were gone but Kathy was sure Sinead was there somewhere. She felt her presence hover around her like the fog.

Kathy walked along the exterior of the grounds,

listening for the voice. She heard it whisper near a wagon, urging her to get closer. When Kathy pulled back the canvas, she was disappointed to find the wagon empty, except for a few stacks of pots and kettles. Kathy tried to frown but she felt her head grow heavy. Perhaps Sinead was hidden behind the pots and kettles? Kathy climbed into the wagon and listened to the small voice that told her to pull the canvas over her body.

"Sinead?" she murmured into the darkness.

Nobody answered. Her eyelids started to drop as the cold clutched her breath. Perhaps she could sleep here through the night and in the morning she would look for Sinead in the other wagons and caravans? Perhaps she was asleep somewhere too, being pulled gently into the night, rocked by the wagon's wheels.

***

Kathy woke as something heavy bumped her head.

"Argh!" she cried, quickly covering her mouth. She pushed the large cast-iron kettle away from her head. She felt foggy and could feel the beginning of a welt on her hairline. Kathy tried to remember how she got into the wagon. She recalled hearing Sinead's voice and then suddenly falling asleep. Kathy felt the damp creep into her bones. She tried to stop her body shivering so she wouldn't disturb the tin pots and make a noise. She clutched the rucksack closer to her body, hoping to keep as much heat in as she could. She heard someone shout about setting up camp nearby. The wagon pulled forward, made a bend to the left and rose up a slight incline. When it stopped, Kathy felt the weight of the driver leave the wagon. She gulped and wedged herself closer to the edge.

Kathy waited for someone to throw the canvas off the wagon but instead, the voices drew farther away. She pulled back the material and squinted at her surroundings. It took a few moments for her eyes to adjust to the reddish dawn that was lighting up the field around them. Kathy groaned. She must be miles away from Ennis and nowhere nearer to Dublin. She pulled back more of the canvas so she could move her head freely to either side. The gypsies from last night were standing together in the centre of the field. The wagon that Kathy was in was just a few feet away from some trees. Carefully, she climbed over the side and dropped onto the soggy grass. She reached over for her rucksack and quickly covered the kettles and pots with the canvas before running off into the trees.

After walking a few metres into the woods, Kathy stopped and leaned against a large elm tree. She rested her forehead against its rough bark and took a deep breath of the morning air. Her nostrils filled with the sweet smell of rain and earth. Birds were singing amidst the tree tops, waking gently to the sunrise. Everything looked tranquil but Kathy couldn't help but feel terrified. She opened the rucksack and pulled out the worn, red wool jumper Sinead had packed. Kathy lifted the jumper to her nose. It smelled of the same damp and dust her own clothes smelled of, but it had the familiar tinge of Sinead. She knew it well from her childhood. Every night they would sneak into one another's bed and curl up together, offering a source of heat and companionship. Kathy would bury her face in Sinead's curly red hair and fall asleep to that comforting smell. They would have continued sharing a bed together if it weren't for the other girls, who started to talk as they got older; implying there was something sinister happening between those sheets.

That and because Kathy had a strange dream one night. One where she was walking down a corridor, and at the very end, there was a door with a key in its lock. She reached for the key, but as she did, it turned into a feather. No matter how hard she pulled, the feather wouldn't leave the lock. Kathy woke up being pushed off the side of the bed with Sinead in tears, shouting that she wanted to pull her hair out. They didn't speak for a week after that.

Kathy felt her stomach churn. Would she ever speak with Sinead again? What if she never made it out of Ennis? Did the nuns catch up to her and bring her back to the orphanage? Sinead was a year younger than Kathy but the girls heard stories of nuns taking misbehaving fifteen-year-olds to the laundries and accidentally tossing their birth certificates, so nothing could be proved otherwise. Kathy pushed the feeling aside. Sinead was clever, she would surely have found a way out.

Kathy hugged the jumper closer to her chest before pulling it over her body. She walked up to a nearby log and sat down. The smell of coffee being brewed and sausages sizzling on an open fire were drifting in the morning air. Her stomach growled. She squinted her eyes at the sun that was rising steadily in the sky. She thought of the other girls and the porridge they would be eating as one unlucky volunteer read out the morning prayer.

Kathy looked down at the forest floor to see if there was anything edible. Just a few feet away was a small bush with berries. She knelt next to it and started to pick the fruit, placing them into her palm. She lifted one up closer for examination. It was bright red. Kathy knew that some berries were poisonous but she couldn't remember what distinguished them from one another. Kathy lifted one to her mouth but dropped it on the ground when she felt something hit her thigh. She jumped back, dropping the rest of the berries, and turned around to find a young man leaning against a nearby tree.

"Do you mind?" he asked with a crooked smile, nodding to the football next to her foot. She wiped the dirt from her knees.

"I do actually, you made me drop my berries," she replied, placing her hands on her hips. The boy's green eyes twinkled as the smile on his lips broadened.

"You should be thanking me so you should, that there is a holly tree and its berries are poisonous," he explained, walking towards her.

Kathy felt her cheeks go red. "Right, er thanks..."

"... Heath."

He bent down and picked up the football as Kathy backed away slowly.

"Right, Heath. I should be going, it's nice to meet you and thanks again for er, saving my life and all."

She looked nervously at the trees toward the camp and picked up her rucksack before turning and walking away.

"Wait, you can't leave now," Heath said, jogging to catch up with her. "You haven't even told me your name."

"I need to go, I'm running late," Kathy said as she started to walk faster.

Heath chuckled. "Running late for what? There's nothing in this direction for miles."

Kathy's stomach dropped.

"All the more reason for me to hurry up," she replied matter-of-factly as she continued to walk in the opposite direction of the camp.

"I guess you could try to get a ride from the road up ahead."

Kathy's steps felt lighter. "Yes, exactly, that's what I'll do."

"But you need somewhere to go first."

"What makes you think I don't have somewhere to go?"

Heath's eyes looked her up and down. Her cheeks reddened.

"You just look like someone who's trying to get away from somewhere, that's all," he said, shrugging and placing his hands in his trouser pockets.

Kathy eyed him suspiciously as she scanned his handsome features; his dishevelled brown hair and his skin darkened from the sun. He wore a wool waistcoat over a white linen shirt that had seen many hours working outside. Kathy stared down at her shiny Oxford shoes. "I'm trying to get to Dublin," she explained, without looking up.

Heath thought about this for a moment, leaning on his left side.

"We're going to Dublin. You could travel with us?" he asked. Kathy met his eyes. She looked ahead at the empty woods and then back at Heath.

"Are you gypsies?" Kathy asked tentatively. She had heard about gypsies before. One of the girls in her orphanage was Romani. The nuns regularly scolded her in front of the others, claiming her father was a thief.

Heath shook his head. "We're Irish Travellers."

"Isn't that the same thing?"

Heath thought about this for a moment. "Sort of, I mean we both travel around but we're from different places I suspect. We have different traditions."

Heath saw a look in Kathy's face. "We're different from what you heard."

"What do you mean?"

"We don't go around stealing things if that's what you're thinking," Heath said, crossing his arms. "Everyone here spends a lot of time practicing talents that we perform for settled people."

Kathy felt her cheeks redden.

"I'm sorry, I didn't mean to offend you." Kathy stared down at her shoes again. "It's just, the nuns at the orphanage told us terrible things about gypsies. I didn't know."

Heath looked her up and down. He uncrossed his arms and put his hands in his pockets again.

"It's okay, we get it a lot. Why are you going to Dublin?"

"I'm meeting a friend. We got separated." Heath frowned. "How did that happen?"

Kathy shook her head. "It's not important. I just need to get there."

Heath nodded. "Like I said, we're going that way. At the very least we could drop you off in a town." He looked at the woods ahead before giving Kathy another crooked smile. "I don't know how well you'd fare out here on your own."

Kathy thought about Sinead. Perhaps she was in the back of a car headed to Dublin already? Kathy needed to get there as soon as possible. She nodded.

"Okay."

"Great, let's get you some breakfast. I wouldn't want you trying to eat hemlock next."

Kathy looked at him, puzzled. He shook his head and chuckled, gesturing for her to follow him back to the camp.

When they reached the edge of the woods, Heath stopped and turned to face her.

"Why don't I go ahead first and bring some stuff back?" Heath asked. "Travellers can be a bit nervous around settled people. I think they'd wonder how one got to their camp if you just walked in from the woods. I'll be right back."

Kathy was about to interject with some kind of protest but Heath had already started walking to the camp before she could say anything. Sighing, Kathy strolled over to an ash tree and leaned against it. She covered her growling stomach with her arms and waited.

After a few minutes, Heath returned with a bread roll in one hand and a mug in another. He handed her the food which she accepted eagerly. Kathy took a bite out of the bread roll and was delighted to find it was stuffed with piping hot sausages. Her mouth salivated at the first bite. It was too hot and burned her tongue but she continued eating it anyway.

"This is delicious!" Kathy exclaimed, bits of food falling from her mouth. Heath laughed.

"Haven't you ever tasted sausages cooked over an open fire?"

She shook her head and stuffed the rest of the bread roll into her mouth. She swallowed the large lump and took a swig of coffee to wash it down.

"We only ever had sausages on Christmas morning and I doubt they were cooked over an open fire."

"That's the only way we cook things here, so you'll get plenty of it." Heath placed his hands in his pockets. "I spoke with Cian on my way back. He's expecting us now." Heath nodded towards the camp. Kathy walked to the edge of the woods with Heath and stopped.

"Are you sure they'll let me stay?"

"I don't think they'd be heartless enough to let someone starve in the woods."

Chapter Two
The Walking People

Heath led Kathy into the field where the caravans were arranged in a spiral, just like in the friary grounds. She caught glimpses of a large inner circle with tents scattered around and people walking about. In the centre was a large, open fire. Heath stopped next to two caravans and edged himself slowly between them. He waved for Kathy to follow before turning left. He approached a yellow door and knocked gently on the wood. Only a few seconds passed before a very tall man appeared, wearing a plaid flat cap. He bent down to look at them both.

"Hullo there, Heath," he said. The tall man moved into the caravan, making room for Heath and Kathy to enter. Heath quickly closed the door behind them.

The interior was just as quaint as the exterior. The walls were painted in an off-white, making the yellow, floral curtains stand out. The man, Kathy assumed to be Cian, moved to the small cast-iron stove underneath the window. He placed a kettle on top of its hot surface. Heath walked up to the white table and gestured for Kathy to take a seat.

The small room was tidy. Everything had its own place. Teacups were arranged in a zigzag pattern, pillows were positioned on each chair, and the bed at the far end of the caravan was neatly made. Kathy smiled at the fluffy duvet embroidered with tiny sunflowers.

Cian poured some boiling water into a teapot, followed by a large heaped spoon of leaves. He set it down abruptly in front of them, spilling water from the spout onto the table. He sat across from Kathy and Heath. Leaning back in his chair, he pulled out a pipe. With a quick light from a match, the caravan filled with the scent of tobacco.

"Which clan are you from?" Cian asked, leaning forward. Kathy opened her mouth to say something but Heath replied, "She's not from a clan."

Cian dropped his pipe into his lap. He jumped up swearing and cursing, trying to brush the hot ashes off as they singed his clothes.

"Jesus, Heath! What the hell are you doing bringing a settled girl in here?" Heath scratched his head nervously, looking over at Kathy apologetically.

"C'mon Cian, she has nowhere to go. I found her in the woods picking poisonous berries to eat." Heath leaned across the table. "Besides, she joined our camp on a full moon. It's bad luck to not let her travel with us until the next moon."

Kathy's cheeks reddened with embarrassment. She wished she could sink into the chair.

Cian sat down again, heaving. He pulled out a small, leather pouch and started to add more tobacco to the top of his pipe. "You're right. But this is reckless, even for you," he continued, shoving the end of the pipe into his mouth. "What will the others think? You can't trust a settled person."

"I don't mean any harm," Kathy interjected. "I'm just trying to get to Dublin."

"How did you get here then? Where are you from girl?"

Kathy stared down at her hands folded in her lap. "Nowhere."

"Don't give me that nonsense. Everyone's gotta be from somewhere," Cian prodded, tapping his pipe on the table.

"Can't we just say she's a Traveller?" Heath countered. "And that she's just trying to get to another clan?"

Cian closed his eyes tightly and rubbed his forehead. He opened them again, looking at Kathy. "You really don't have any way of getting to Dublin yourself?" he asked softly.

She shook her head.

Cian leaned in closer to Kathy and Heath. "If we're going to do this, then you both need to keep it to yourselves." He looked at them with tired, brown eyes. "We'll fulfil our moon promise and shelter you until next month. After that, we'll drop you off in the nearest town."

"Can't we take her to Dublin with us?" Heath asked. Cian leaned back on his chair and adjusted the pipe to the side of his mouth.

"You know that's not a decision I can make. We have strict rules. No settlers and only Travellers with special talents can stay with us. Everyone's gotta earn their keep and we've more than enough siders to keep this camp running." He nodded as he swiped a match and brought its flame to the end of his pipe. He inhaled in quick successions before waving the match in the air to extinguish it.

"But if she had a talent," Heath began, smiling at Kathy. "She could stay?"

Cian waved his hand and inhaled deeply into his pipe. "Off you go, the both of ye. I've done all I can." Heath winked at Kathy before standing up to leave.

They left their untouched mugs of tea and walked across the room. Heath opened the door of the caravan and stepped out into the warm air, with Kathy by his side.

"How many Travellers live here?" Kathy asked, observing the chaos in front of her. Horses were being walked while people were standing and chatting, carrying dishes or baskets filled with produce. Dogs were growling and chasing each other, and a small cat sat on the roof of the oldest caravan.

"There are six couples, an elder and seven of us young people."

"And you all have your own caravans?"

"Nah, only the married couples and Laoise, our elder, have caravans. I share a tent with three other lads."

"You don't live with your parents?"

"I don't have parents. None of us do."

"You're an orphan too?" Kathy asked.

Heath nodded. "I guess you could say that. I've never felt like an orphan. Especially with Cian and his wife, Sloane. They've always treated me as their own."

Kathy looked down at her shoes that were now covered in mud. Heath took a deep breath and stretched his arms above his head.

"So Traveller girl, who would you like to meet first?" he asked with a crooked grin. Kathy smiled shyly.

"It'd be nice to meet the people I'm sharing a caravan with," she suggested.

Heath nodded and looked away. "Suppose that makes sense. Fair warning, the girls aren't the friendliest. It's best to keep out of their way." He strode ahead of Kathy to the centre of the caravans. The fire was burning brightly and two women were bent over a large tin tub filled with suds. The thin woman scrubbed dishes while the plump one stood over her making sharp remarks. Heath looked back.

"I'd wait for a quieter time to introduce yourself to the cooks. Especially Courtney. She gets in a foul mood on arrival mornings."

Heath and Kathy quickly moved on and, as if on cue, they heard shouting from the plump one as they walked away. Heath walked past two more caravans before standing outside a brightly coloured one that was lined with a red trim. The wheels were the same height as Kathy, making the small set of stairs leading to the porch necessary to reach the door. Heath climbed up the steps and was about to knock on the yellow painted door but a voice called from behind him.

"Heath, what are you doing?"

Kathy looked behind her and saw a tall, slender woman with a stern face.

"Hi Sloane, I was introducing Kathy here to the rest of the girls." Sloane looked at Kathy.

"And who is Kathy?" Sloane asked, eyeing her up. Heath ran down the small wooden steps and walked to Kathy's side. She felt his arm graze against hers.

"She's just another Traveller who lost her parents. They dropped her off in Ennis."

"Is that so? Cian didn't tell me and I'd be surprised if Laoise knows." Sloane peered sharply at Kathy, her piercing look eyed her up and down.

"What clan did you say you were from girl?" Sloane asked.

Kathy crossed her left arm, covering her elbow. "Uhm..."

"She's from the Sharron clan," Heath interjected. Sloane reached out and pulled on Heath's right ear making him shout and bend forward.

"Don't lie to me boy. Let's go, the pair of you." Sloane walked to the giant fire with Heath stumbling at her heels while she kept hold of his ear. They approached the old caravan Kathy spotted earlier. The cat stared as the three of them approached. It crossed its paws and yawned.

"We don't need to bother Laoise about this. Just ask Cian, he'll tell you!"

"I don't really believe that now do I?"

Sloane walked up to the door, forcing Heath to climb up the steps behind her. She tapped gently against its old frame and waited with Heath behind. He looked up at Kathy and mouthed an apology. Kathy stood awkwardly, her arms against her chest.

She looked around her. People were starting to stare at the interaction between Sloane and Heath. They were starting to notice Kathy. Some began to point and whisper. Had she been found out already? Kathy felt her chest tighten. The few seconds they waited for that door to open felt like an eternity. When it did, Kathy felt a wave of relief. Inside the caravan was an old, short woman. Her white hair floated around her face in curls and her eyes were magnified by a large pair of turquoise spectacles.

"Hello Sloane, it's nice to see you," Laoise said. "And you brought Heath with you too, I see," she added, looking behind Sloane.

"Hullo Laoise," Heath mumbled.

"Heath brought a gorger back with him from Ennis," Sloane said sharply, looking back at Kathy. "He claims she's a Traveller from the Sharron clan."

Laoise looked at Kathy for a moment before replying, "Yes, that's right."

"That's right?" Sloane asked in disbelief.

"Yes, she's from the Sharron clan, it's..."

"Kathy," Heath added. Sloane pulled harder on his ear, making him curse under his breath.

"Yes, that's right, Kathy." Laoise stepped onto the landing outside her door. Sloane moved out of her way, releasing Heath's ear in the process. Laoise climbed down the steps and approached Kathy. Her long black dress dragged on the ground behind her. She reached out her wrinkled hand which was weighed down by large rings that adorned each finger. Kathy accepted her cool embrace.

"Yes, Kathy from the Sharron clan. It's very nice to meet you in person."

Kathy nodded, too stunned to speak. Sloane walked down the steps quickly, joining Laoise by her side. She avoided the faces in the crowd, which were now smirking.

"I'm sorry Laoise, I didn't realise you knew."

Laoise let go of Kathy's hand and turned around. "I don't make a point to notify you of very much, so I'm not surprised."

Laoise walked up the steps to her caravan, placing a ringed hand upon Heath's shoulder. "I'd put some wet moss on that ear, it'll bring down the swelling," she said before returning to her caravan and closing the door behind her.

Sloane stalked off before either of them could speak, her eyes focused on the ground. Heath walked over to Kathy's side.

"I'm sorry about that, Kathy. I had no idea she'd make such a fuss about it," Heath explained, rubbing his ear and wincing.

"That's okay, at least this means I can stay now, doesn't it?"

Heath nodded. "Yeah, guess it does."

The Travellers who had been watching the scene unfold started to approach.

Kathy smiled faintly, feeling overwhelmed as Heath introduced her to the different families. There were the O'Sullivan's; Paddy the fiddler and Nora, the palm reader. They both greeted her with big smiles, clasping her hands in theirs and wishing she would bring them a new talent. There was Bree, who held out an awkward hand for her to shake, before tripping against her husband Niall as they walked away. Heath briefly introduced Kathy to the Keating's but Courtney, the plump cook, stormed off impatiently soon after, while Leary stood scratching his head and apologising. Kathy looked around at the friendly faces that greeted her enthusiastically. As she was meeting all these people, she couldn't help but think that the one face she wanted to see wasn't there. Her stomach sank thinking of Sinead. Would Kathy get to Dublin in time?

Heath leaned over and whispered, "Are you okay? You look a bit pale."

"Yeah, it's all just a bit much really."

Thankfully a clanging of wood against tin reverberated throughout the camp. Everyone turned their heads from Kathy and walked to the fire where Courtney and Bree were pouring soup into tin bowls. Kathy looked over to the line of people crowded around the fire, talking and laughing. She felt out of place and covered her stomach with her arms.

"Why don't you head into the woods? I'll bring us some soup if you like?" Heath asked.

Kathy nodded gratefully. She turned around and walked past the red- trimmed caravan she was now expected to call home for the next month and into the woods. She found a clearing and sat on a large rock next to a tree. She burrowed her head between her knees and felt hot tears sting her cheeks. A few moments later, Heath appeared carrying two steaming bowls of soup.

"What's wrong Kathy?" Heath set the bowls of soup on the ground and sat next to her on the rock.

"Sorry, it's just a lot. I wish Sinead were here."

Kathy wiped the tears from her cheek with the sleeve of her jumper.

"Where's your friend now?"

"I'm not sure, we were supposed to catch a ride from Ennis to Dublin together but we had to split up. We agreed to meet at the friary but she never came."

"She could be on her way to Dublin right now but she could also still be back in Ennis, or worse."

Kathy's eyes filled once more with tears. Heath nudged himself closer so he was almost touching her. "I'm sure she's finding her own way to Dublin, I mean you did, right?"

Kathy nodded and wiped more tears from her face.

"I'd hate to think what they'd do to her if they caught her."

Heath looked down at his own bowl and shook his head.

"That sounds awful, being locked up like that."

Kathy didn't say anything, instead she bent forward and picked up a bowl of soup. She looked down at the green watercress floating in the stock. She stirred the contents and shakily brought a spoon to her mouth.

"How's your ear?" Kathy asked quietly.

"It's alright. Could be worse." Heath leaned forward to grab his own bowl and started to tuck into his food.

"Sloane has a temper."

"I've noticed," Kathy mumbled darkly. "She's not that bad, honest."

Kathy raised her eyebrow. "I'll believe it when I see another side of her."

Heath shrugged and continued eating his soup.

Kathy heard the scrape of metal as she reached the bottom of her bowl. She set it on the ground and wiped her mouth with her sleeve. She looked up at the sky, a few clouds were starting to drift over them.

"So, what is all this talk about a talent?" Kathy asked, still looking up at the sky.

"We have a rule here for people who want to join us. It's so we always have a way to make an income and ensure we can feed people."

"What's the rule?"

"Everyone that's part of our clan has to have a talent to perform at our Midnight Circus. It needs to be good too because we have a reputation and people come across the country to be entertained. We need to keep it up, you know."

"What's your talent?"

Heath smiled, moving his brown hair from his eyes. "I play the fiddle."

Kathy smiled. "I'm impressed, we never learned to play instruments at school." She looked down at her hands and imagined what it would feel like to make music from them.

Kathy and Heath spent the rest of the afternoon talking and walking in the woods. Heath explained what it was like to perform in front of people and how it was something they all looked forward to each month.

They talked for so long they missed their supper. The sun was setting when they finally walked back to the camp. Heath escorted her to the caravan where Kathy would be staying, and waited as she climbed up the steps. She could hear voices coming from the other side of the door. Kathy turned before opening it.

"See you tomorrow?"

Heath gave her a crooked smile. "Sweet dreams," he whispered before walking off to his tent.

Kathy took a deep breath and opened the door. As soon as she did, the voices stopped. She walked in and found three girls sitting on a bed across the room, staring up at her. The one in the middle smiled amusingly, as she ran her hand through her blonde hair that flowed over a pale blue silk scarf wrapped around her neck.

"So, you're the new girl then?" she asked.

Kathy nodded awkwardly looking around the interior of the caravan. It was small but managed to fit two bunk beds inside. On either side of these beds was a chest, presumably where everyone kept their possessions. In the centre of the room was a small table and fluffy pillows around it. To the side, a cast-iron oven, keeping the room warm.

"Close the door; it's draughty enough in here," snapped the dark-haired girl. She walked over and opened the oven door, throwing two logs inside before closing it quickly.

"Who is she?" asked the brunette girl.

"Just a girl Heath's rebounded with," the blonde

girl replied, smirking.

"My name is Kathy," Kathy responded cooly, moving closer to the wood stove to warm her hands. The blonde girl tossed her hair back.

"We don't have enough beds. You'll have to share with Kira." She looked over to the bed with a mass of black hair tucked under the duvet.

"Good luck. You might find yourself turned into a frog in the morning," the dark-haired one added, making the brunette laugh.

Kathy rolled her eyes and mumbled a sarcastic thanks. She removed her red jumper and folded it carefully on top of the chest. She removed her shoes and stockings before crawling under the blankets. She tried to ignore the whispers and giggling from the three girls by focusing on the little girl's steady breathing next to her. Kathy closed her eyes and fought back burning tears. She inhaled slowly and imagined all the places Sinead could be at that moment.

Chapter Three
The Fiddler

When she woke up late the next morning, to Kathy's relief, the caravan was empty. She looked around the room while rubbing her eyes. The old furniture and wood panels seemed different with the sunlight pouring onto them. Outside, Kathy heard a thudding sound near the caravan. She pulled back the duvet and let her feet drop on the cold wood floor. She found her stockings she had laid out the night before and pulled them on. Taking her time, she slipped her feet into her shoes and tied the laces. Would Heath be waiting for her? She wondered this as she pulled Sinead's red, wool jumper over her head.

Kathy took a deep breath and opened the door.

The morning sunlight hit her eyes, forcing her to mask her face with her hand. Cautiously, she stepped down the steps and looked around at her surroundings. Kathy noticed that their caravan was positioned on the outskirts of the camp. It was quiet here, with no one around. Aside from the birds singing, she could hear the same light thuds she heard in the caravan. Kathy walked around it and smiled as she watched Heath kick his football and nudge it with his head, before continuing again.

"Ah, there you are!" Heath exclaimed, grabbing the football, before running up to her.

"I was wondering when you'd wake up. Unfortunately, you've gone and slept through breakfast." He said, scratching his head awkwardly.

Kathy smiled. "I'm not very hungry, I'm just glad to see you came back."

"Of course I've come back. Let's get going, I want to introduce you to some people."

Heath walked Kathy around the outer circle of the caravans. He pointed out which caravan belonged to whom. Though the names sounded familiar, she couldn't picture their faces.

"Don't worry Kath, you'll get to know them all soon."

"Sinead calls me that," Kathy said sadly.

"Do you mind if I call you that too?"

"No, it's nice. It reminds me of her."

"It's just through here." Heath pointed to an area with some horses grazing. They walked past a small caravan. Outside sat the same little girl Kathy slept next to. She was sitting on a woman's lap.

"Who is that?" Kathy asked as the short, dark woman began to plait the young girl's hair. She was humming gently as her hands quickly criss-crossed each other. Heath frowned.

"The young one is named Kira. And that's Mary, she makes jewellery now and helps with the cleaning, but she used to be a great singer. People would come from all over to hear her songs. About five years ago, she went for a walk and came back hours after sunset with a look about her. She refused to sing again. She just hums the same song over and over."

Heath looked back at the woman before leaning in to whisper, "They say, when she went walking that evening, she must have passed a fairy hill after sunset and heard the good people play their harp. That the song she heard marked her heart and haunts her every day." Heath ran his hand through his hair. "I suppose that's why Kira came to us that autumn after. They gave her a child of their own, so she can teach her their song."

Kathy looked back to Kira on her lap. "You think Kira's a changeling?"

Heath nodded. "Ay, that child is touched. It's as if she doesn't belong to this world. I guess that's why she doesn't speak either." He paused, looking back at them for a second. "Of course, there's nothing wrong with them. She's a sweet child well enough but she just doesn't belong here."

Heath turned away and walked up to the group of grazing horses. Next to them was a short boy with sandy hair. The lad was busying himself with saddling a white horse.

"How's the craic, Kieran," Heath called, raising his hand. The sandy-haired boy turned and gave him a nod, chewing something on the side of his mouth. Heath approached him and reached his arm out for the white horse to smell his hand.

"She's ready for you now, Heath," the boy replied, patting the horse's thigh. Kathy looked up at the majestic creature. She felt tiny as it towered above her head.

"Kath, this is Kieran," Heath nodded to the boy.

Kathy reached out her hand to shake his. Instead, he kept them in his trousers pockets and nodded while looking at the ground.

Heath laughed and turned to Kathy. "Kieran here prefers the company of horses to that of men or women." Kieran shuffled his feet and spat some black stuff on the ground. He wrapped his thumbs around his braces.

"Bring her back before dusk," he said between his chewing before walking off to attend to a tabby horse. Heath tipped his flat cap and stepped up to the reigns. He threw his right leg over the horse and settled into the leather saddle. He leaned down on one side and stuck out his hand.

"You want me to get up on that?" Kathy asked, stunned.

"'Course. If you're gonna be a Traveller, Kath, you need to learn how to ride like one." Kathy looked down at her pleated skirt.

"You'll be fine. Trust me." He inched his hand closer to hers. She sighed and mumbled under her breath.

"Put your left foot in that reign there. Just like that Now take my hand."

Kathy fit her small hand into his and felt the roughness of his skin against hers. His touch made her heart beat quicker. He pulled her up and she wrapped her right leg around the horse, settling herself into the saddle.

"Hold tight," he instructed as he kicked the horse on its side. The horse began to trot away from camp.

Kathy leaned forward, wrapping her arms around Heath's waist. The horse bounced them up and down as it galloped. The motion made Kathy feel like she was going to fall off at any moment. She closed her eyes and tried not to think about the height between her and the ground. Heath kicked the horse into a faster gallop.

"We're going through the woods now. Keep your head low." Kathy did as she was told and closed her eyes tightly. She pressed her forehead against his muscular back.

"Okay, we're out now. Take a look!"

Kathy opened her eyes and gasped at the sight. They were at the top of a hill. All around her for miles were lush green slopes rolling into one another. It took her breath away. She closed her eyes and felt the cool breeze against her skin, the air smelled sweet.

"Where am I?" she asked, her eyes bright. "You're in Ireland," Heath chuckled, looking back at her.

"This isn't the Ireland I know." She pressed herself closer to his back to keep warm against the wind that gusted around them.

"There's a lot more to see." Heath kicked the horse again and galloped down the hill and into a valley. Kathy listened to the horse's hooves stamp against the damp grass. When they reached the bottom of the valley, Heath hopped off. Kathy slid down the side awkwardly, while Heath caught her by the waist. She stumbled into his chest and quickly moved back.

"Sorry," Kathy stammered, looking down, her cheeks blushing. What would the nuns think of her now? She looked around, at the mounds of emerald green coming up to greet the blue sky. Kathy pulled her jumper closer to her body.

"You must have seen so many amazing places," Kathy said, looking up at the hills in the distance.

"We see a lot but sometimes it all looks the same." From the corner of her eye, she saw Heath's gaze float down from her wavy hair to her waist. He snapped his attention back to the white horse and leaned against it. His hand perched on her side.

"I'm gonna be sad to see this one go," he said, as he stroked her white mane.

"Why does she have to go?" Kathy asked, stroking her back thigh.

"She's a thoroughbred. Been trained to be a racehorse you see. She'll do well at the horse fair, won't you Rosie?"

"You train horses?"

Heath shook his head. "Kieran does, alongside Tommy. They know what to look for when buying a foal. Kieran's got a good eye."

Kathy leaned against the horse and looked up at the dark cloud that was moving over them. "Do you sell them at the Midnight Circus?"

Heath shook his head. "Nah, we just do horse riding for kids and stuff. Come August, we bring them to a big horse show and sell our best ones."

The wind picked up. Small drops of water fell and began to dampen the grass. Kathy laughed, looking up at the sky. She closed her eyes and felt the rain against her face.

"Let's go, we'll catch our death if we don't get back. It looks like a storm is coming." Heath climbed up onto the horse and lent his hand for Kathy to join him. They rode back to the camp while the rain steadily picked up. Kathy kept her eyes closed for the journey and felt the embrace of the wind on her body. When they reached the other horses in camp, the rain was torrential. It was so heavy they couldn't see anything. Heath stepped down and lifted his hand to help Kathy. When she jumped down, Heath slipped on the mud and they toppled on top of each other. Kathy laughed as Heath laid on his back with his flat cap over his face.

Kathy pulled the hat from his face and said, "Not so confident now, are we?"

"Get off," he mumbled, embarrassed.

Kathy moved over and lifted her face up to the clouds. She opened her palms and felt the rain against her hands. She looked over to Heath and saw he was watching her. He reached his hand to move a wet strand of her auburn hair from her face. He moved his face closer. Kathy felt her heart beat fast, as something inside her stomach clenched.

"Oi, Heath!" Kieran called, running toward them and picking up Rosie's reigns from the wet ground.

"What are you doing down there?"

Kathy and Heath pulled apart and quickly stood up from the ground. Kathy tried to wipe the mud from her legs and skirt.

"You both need to dry off before you catch your death," Kieran called, as he walked Rosie back to the others. Kathy looked at the ground, embarrassed.

"He's right, we should get back to the camp," Heath said, looking away. His cheeks burned a bright a red.

"Yeah, you're right. Let's dry ourselves."

***

They said goodbye at the girls' caravan. Kathy stood outside while the last few raindrops fell on her already soaked hair. Heath walked away, his flat cap pulled down to cover his face, both hands in pockets.

Kathy opened the caravan door and stepped inside. She was happy to see that it was still empty. She pulled off her wet clothes and laid them on the laundry line near the cast-iron stove. She opened her rucksack and looked for her extra pair of knickers and the wool dress she packed. She pulled out the wool socks Sinead brought with her. Kathy held them in her hands and quickly stuffed them back into her bag. It didn't feel right to wear them. What if they met on the road and Sinead needed the socks herself?

Kathy dressed quickly and looked at herself in the full- length mirror, on the other side of the caravan. She frowned at her reflection. Kathy remembered how jealous she used to feel whenever she watched Sinead getting dressed. Kathy ran her hands up her small hips and waist, to her small firm breasts. She always felt uncomfortable with her boyish figure. She frowned at the sight of her knobbly knees. She thought of Heath on the ground and watched as her cheeks turned a deep burgundy. She brought her hand to her face and felt the warmth from it. Could he ever like someone like her?

Kathy tried to comb through her knotted hair but it stuck together against her body. She sighed and turned to put on her shoes. They were still wet and squishy from earlier. Kathy wished she brought another pair with her.

She left the caravan and walked to the camp's centre fire. Standing next to it was the large plump woman named Courtney, who Kathy met the day before. She walked over, thinking the least she could do was to offer her help in preparing meals.

"You must be the new girl," Courtney snapped, as Kathy approached. The plump woman hammered her knuckles into a slab of thick dough.

"Er... we met yesterday... I just wanted to see if you needed any help." Kathy said timidly.

"Speak up girl. I can't hear a thing with that mumbling."

"Do you need help?" Kathy asked again.

"Help? Help would have been telling me in advance that we have another mouth to feed. No one seems to give a damn how their food ends up on their plates as long as it does." She slammed the dough against the tree stump she was using as a counter-top.

"Go and help Bree make the coffee," Courtney instructed, looking over to an awkward, thin woman struggling to place the small black beans into a metal grinder.

Kathy nodded nervously and walked up to Bree. She was about to offer some help, but before she could, Courtney charged past, pushing Kathy to the side, and shouted, "Mind the kettle, Bree!"

Courtney walked over to where the younger woman was sitting. She grabbed the cast-iron kettle from the fire's embers with such a force that it caused boiling water to splash onto the fire. Bree looked up with a sheepish grin, her hands awkwardly rubbing against her soot-stained skin. She stood as a child would, anticipating some form of punishment for her misdemeanor. Instead, Courtney gave her an exasperated look before turning on her heels and marching away, shaking her head. Kathy backed away. She turned from the fire and found Heath walking in the other direction.

"Oh, Heath, wait up!"

Heath turned and smiled. "I was just about to see Paddy. He has a new song he wants to teach me." Kathy hurried toward him.

Heath looked back. "What was that all about?"

"I tried to help Bree make coffee."

"Ah," Heath replied, raising his eyebrow. They walked until they saw a tall man leaning against his caravan, tuning his fiddle and whistling.

"Alright Heath?" he called, as the two approached. Heath nodded.

"Paddy, you remember Kathy?"

"Course I do. We met the other day. Pleasure to see you again, Kathy." Paddy said, reaching out to shake her hand. Kathy placed her small hand in his and felt her arm rise and fall as he shook it vigorously. Kathy pulled her hand back and rubbed her wrist.

"Nice to see you too."

"I guess you're here to watch our Heath prepare for the next Midnight Circus?"

Kathy nodded. "Do you mind?"

"Not at all, Heath needs to learn how to keep his focus," he said, tapping Heath on the shoulder with the fiddle's bow and winking.

"Right then Heath, let's pick up from yesterday. Grab yer fiddle, Kathy and I will take a seat here along this log and you'll enchant us with yer music." He winked before walking over to the log and sitting on its mossy surface. He stretched out his long legs and leaned back with his hands on his head.

"You're in for a treat miss," he said, nodding as Heath came back around the caravan. In his arms, he carried an old fiddle. Paddy nodded and closed his eyes. Heath cleared his throat and placed the fiddle on his left shoulder. He closed his eyes and started to play. His left hand trembled over the strings, while his right hand directed the bow. The song was sad but the notes were beautiful. One by one, they washed over Kathy. It was only when the last note drifted into silence that she realised her eyes were watering.

"Well done my boy, well done," Paddy said, nodding with approval.

"Now let's liven up the music, shall we?" He reached behind the log and grabbed his own fiddle. "One-two-three," he said, and they were off. The song made Heath move with his whole body. The music streamed from his fingers and his feet.

At the end of three duets and a complicated new piece that made Heath stumble a few times, Paddy called it a day and patted Heath on the head.

Kathy clapped loudly.

"I'm impressed!" she said, as Heath took a bow.

"I was born with a fiddle."

"Really?"

"Yup," he looked down at the instrument. "It was the only thing I have left of my parents. I was told my da' was a great fiddler. That this belonged to him," he said, lifting the fiddle so Kathy could see its weathered body. It certainly looked older than Heath. She smiled and reached for the cross around her neck and thought of the old paperback book that was under her pillow.

She knew what it was like to only have a few things left behind from your parents.

"You know, I meant it when I said we can try to find you a talent too. That way you can travel to Dublin with us."

Kathy thought about this for a moment. She looked down at her shoes and wondered where Sinead was. Dublin was still miles away and Kathy had no other way of getting there on her own.

"Okay," she said slowly. "But I don't think we're going to discover a hidden talent. I was never particularly good at anything in school."

Heath laughed and gave her a crooked smile. He leaned in and whispered, "You've been to school, so that already makes you more special than the rest of us."

She smiled shyly and shook her head.

"I'm sure we can find something you like. There are tons of talents here," Heath explained, looking over to the centre of the camp. Kathy shrugged her shoulders, unconvinced.

"Sure, let's try."

The two of them went for their supper. While they sat side by side, their knees touching each other, they plotted all the different talents Kathy could try over the next few weeks.

"Which one should I try first?"

"The fiddle, of course. You already have an amazing teacher for that one."

Kathy snorted into her empty bowl.

"I'm ready for bed," Heath said, looking up at the pink sky and stretching out his arms. Kathy felt a pang in her stomach. She was enjoying her time with him. That and she was nervous to go back to the caravan with the other girls.

"They're probably in the woods drinking whiskey now," Heath commented, seeing the look on Kathy's face. Kathy nodded, she wrapped her arms around her stomach.

"Good. They're pretty mean, you know."

Heath frowned. "I know, I'm sorry."

Heath waved good night to Kathy before heading in the direction of his tent. Kathy walked slowly to her caravan, hoping that the other girls weren't inside just yet. When she opened the door, Kathy was relieved to find the only one inside the caravan was Kira. The little girl sat on their shared bed, looking through a small, leaf filled wooden box on her lap. She looked up at Kathy and smiled before picking up a leaf and examining it closely. Kathy sat next to her on their bed.

"Are these from all the places you've been to?" Kathy asked quietly, looking at a yellow leaf. Kira nodded.

"They're beautiful." Kira looked up at Kathy and smiled before picking up another leaf from her box.

"My name's Kathy by the way." The little girl smiled up at her.

"And I was told that your name is Kira?" Kathy asked, hoping the girl would respond with something other than silence. She just looked up, nodded and returned to her leaves.

I guess Heath was right, Kathy thought to herself. Perhaps she is a changeling. Kathy gently stroked the top of Kira's head and asked, "Would you like me to plait your hair?"

Kira nodded and smiled. She pointed at two brightly coloured bands on the bedside table next to a brush. Kathy took the brush and ran it through Kira's thick, dark hair. It reminded her of Sinead, who had hair just as thick as hers. She'd wear it in two plaits and in the morning wavy curls would surround her freckled face. The girls would fight over who'd get to run their brushes through her hair. It was so thick and after just a few strokes, it turned into a beautiful, shiny mane. Kathy sighed as she ran the brush through Kira's hair.

After Kathy created two identical plaits. They got under their fluffy shared duvet. Kathy pulled out the old paperback book from the rucksack under the bed. She looked over to Kira, who was staring wide-eyed at the wooden ceiling.

"Would you like me to read you a story?" Kathy asked. Kira nodded. Kathy pulled back the book cover. It bent easily, as it had all those other nights, and Kathy read the start of the book as she'd done so many times before.

***

That night, Kathy fell into a restless dream. When she opened her eyes, she saw Kira sitting next to her, her hair plaited. They were sitting on top of a mound. The grass was soft and the ground was warm. The hill swelled with the sunlight that hid behind purple clouds. Kira was pointing to the paperback book in her lap and was telling Kathy a story. Kathy turned to look at the child. She had the same dark eyes and hair.

"You have to follow the words if you want to tell the story," Kira said. Kathy looked closer at the box in Kira's lap. The words were moving across the page, chasing one another.

"How do you keep up with them?" Kathy asked.

Kira gently tapped her index finger on the page and they started to vibrate.

"It's going to rain soon," Kira said, looking up at the purple sky. "The pages don't like to get wet." Kira stood up quickly and ran down the hill.

"Kira, wait up!" Kathy called. She tried to chase after Kira, but as she placed her hand onto the ground to push herself up, it started to sink. Kathy looked around her, panicking. She was being swallowed by the hill.

"Kira wait!" Kathy cried as she struggled to pick herself out of the sinking hill. Kira looked back and smiled.

Chapter Four
The Book of Moons

Kathy woke with a jolt. The paperback book she had been reading the night before slipped off her body, hitting the floor with a thud. She sat up quickly. Her heart hammered against her chest while she waited for her eyes to adjust to the morning light. She looked over at the bunk bed across the room. The blonde haired girl was snoring lightly, as the black haired one above her turned over. Kathy looked next to her and found the space Kira slept in last night was empty. She quickly pulled on her stockings and shoes and slipped out of the caravan.

Kathy walked up to the large fire. She crouched near the flames and held out her hands. Heath walked up to her, stretching and yawning.

"Morning," he said, taking a seat on the earth next to her. "Sleep well?"

She shook her head, still looking into the flames.

"I had the strangest dream last night," Kathy said, trailing off as she looked into the fire. She tried to remember what it was about but the images were slipping from her mind.

"I don't feel very safe with the others."

"That bad huh?"

Kathy shrugged. "I've met nicer people."

"Yeah, the girls can be pretty terrible."

"I would have thought they'd be nicer to you, since you've known them for a while."

Heath looked up as the blonde haired girl with the blue silk scarf around her neck walked up to the fire. She leaned against the table while Bree ground the coffee beans. His eyes flickered back to Kathy.

"That blonde one, Birgitta, we had a thing for a bit and it didn't work out," he explained, nodding in her direction. "So now Moira and Fallon hate me."

"Oh, right."

"It was nothing serious," Heath added, looking up at Kathy.

"I'm sorry, it doesn't sound like it ended well."

"It didn't, doesn't make it easy either when you share close quarters," he sighed, looking around the camp.

"Have you ever thought about leaving?"

"All the time. I'm saving up to get a horse at the Lughnasadh fair in August."

"That soon, huh?" Kathy asked, her stomach tightening.

"Yeah, but I'd also like to go to Dublin, so I suppose it might make sense to stick around until we get closer."

Kathy tried to hold back her smile. "Yeah, of course."

They sat by the fire in silence, staring into the flames. Kathy raised her head as Courtney carried a tall silver pot with steam coming from the spout.

"That smells incredible," Kathy said as Courtney started to pour the dark, velvety liquid into mugs on a silver tray. Kathy was about to stand up but Heath grabbed her arm.

"What are you doing?" he whispered. She lowered herself again. "You can't just grab a cup, Courtney hands them out." Kathy looked confused.

"But we're the first ones here this morning, shouldn't we get it first?"

"Not likely, unless you're a tarot reader."

"I don't understand?"

Heath rolled his eyes. "It's one of our rituals. We serve the coffee by a ranking."

"What kind of ranking?"

"Based on talents. Tarot readers first, then palm readers, then musicians and dancers and then..."

"People like Mary?" she asked. Heath looked down.

"There's nothing wrong with being a sider."

"Sider?" Kathy asked in disbelief.

"Yeah, people who help take care of the horses and organise the Midnight Circuses."

Kathy nodded and watched Courtney stand with a single mug in her hand. The old woman, named Laoise, emerged from her tattered caravan. Most people in the camp who were making their way to the fire started to create a semi-circle around Courtney and the coffee.

"That's the woman who lied for me, isn't it?" Kathy whispered into Heath's ear. Heath nodded and shushed her.

Laoise's silver hair was pulled back into a low bun and her eyes were framed with turquoise spectacles. Everyone stood silently as she glided to the front of the crowd and reached out her small hand to accept the coffee. Laoise stood for a moment staring into the cup. She breathed in the aromas before taking a long sip of the beverage. Slowly, Laoise turned and walked through the crowd. Everyone stood back and made a clear path to her caravan's orange, paint chipped door. It was only once the door closed that the rest of the crowd began to form a queue and, one by one, accepted the mugs of coffee handed to them.

"She must be important then?" Kathy asked, as they moved to the back of the queue.

"She's the oldest Traveller and she's a tarot reader."

Kathy looked back at the old caravan. "Why does she keep her door closed?" she whispered.

"I don't know; she's always done so," Heath said, moving his hands to his trouser pockets.

Heath and Kathy waited until everyone accepted their mug of coffee before receiving their own. Kathy looked down at her cup. Dregs from the bottom of the coffee pot were floating on the surface. She tasted the lukewarm coffee and sighed. It was thick and surprisingly bitter. It would have tasted better if it had been hot. She looked up at the orange door, wondering why the old woman allowed Kathy to stay with the Travellers.

***

After breakfast, Kathy decided to take a walk down to the river. The smell of damp cedar wood and rain filled her nostrils as she squeezed between two caravans. Kathy spotted Kira holding tightly onto Mary's hand.

Kira waved as Kathy walked over.

"You must be Kathy," the dark woman smiled brightly, reaching over to give Kathy a hug.

"Kira's excited to have some company. Those other girls aren't too kind to the poor child," she explained, clicking her tongue. She reached down and smoothed the stray hairs on top of Kira's head. Kira looked up with her dark eyes and smiled.

"I'm Mary, Mary Collins. You might have seen my husband Tommy, he takes care of the horses and the like."

Kathy smiled shyly. "It's nice to meet you."

"So what brings you to our camp? Have ye got a special talent?"

Kathy's cheeks blushed. She crossed her arms against her chest and shook her head.

"Never mind that, we have plenty of them. What we need is more people like Courtney and Bree," Mary said, nodding to the two women walking up from the river. Both ladies were carrying pales of water on either side of their hips. Bree tripped over her own feet and sloshed some water down her brown dress. Courtney looked back and made a comment that made Bree take a step back from her.

"Bless them," Mary said, shaking her head. "They keep this camp running. If it weren't for them we'd have all starved by now. But it's never enough for people." Mary bent down and picked up Kira. She bounced the child on her hip and continued, "It ain't right, having just a few of us to do the labour and the like. But all them with their talents, they think they're the ones keeping the camp together." Mary shook her head and, as if coming back from a trance, she looked back at Kathy and smiled. "But never mind all that, we're pleased to have you Kathy. Drop by my caravan anytime, we can use the help with beading and the like."

Kathy smiled and waved as they walked between the caravans back into the camp, while Mary hummed and played with Kira's hair.

***

Kathy spent the next few days following her new routine of waking up early and meeting Heath. They'd walk to the fire for their breakfast and watch as the people crowded around them to receive their first morning coffee. It always began with the old woman, Laoise. She would emerge from her caravan, look over them with her large turquoise spectacles, and after taking one sip, she'd carry the cup back to her home.

Whenever Kathy walked past Laoise's caravan, she'd slow down and try to peek through the curtains. But they were always drawn closed. Kathy never heard a sound coming from the caravan; except for that of a kettle or sometimes the long coughing fits that usually came about in the evenings and mornings. Often, she'd get a whiff of incense creeping through the glass panes or underneath the door.

Laoise kept to herself, except for every other morning, when she'd sit outside on a large wooden chair, nursing her second cup of coffee. She'd wait for Birgitta to emerge from her hangover to learn something new about tarot. They'd lay their cards out on a small crate and Laoise would point to the different parts on the cards. Birgitta would lean in intensely, her eyes wide and eager to learn.

Fallon and Moira spent these mornings with a very stout woman named Nora. They sat around a round table under a canopy that extended from her green caravan. They'd spend the hours chatting and laughing over tea. Pausing every now and then to look at something on their palms. Heath spent most of his mornings with Paddy, where he continued to learn new songs and perfect the old ones. Kathy liked to watch him from a distance. It made her feel unseen and gave her an opportunity to really look at him without his eyes meeting hers. She loved the way his whole body moved with the songs. How his left foot would beat against the ground while his right rooted him to the earth. She liked the way a brown curl would fall onto his brow, while his head lolled to the music. It amazed Kathy that the camp, which appeared chaotic at first, was actually organised, even without clocks. They all knew when they had to be somewhere, and they all had somewhere to be.

One day, after lunch, Heath and Kathy went to the patch of grazing grass they called the stables, to help Kieran with the horses. On their way there, Mary and Kira bumped into them.

"Kathy, good to see you!" Mary beamed pulling Kathy into a hug.

Kathy smiled awkwardly and nodded. "You too."

Mary looked over to Heath and gave him a short nod before returning to Kathy.

"I'm glad we found you. Kira was hoping to spend some time with you and I need to get to my beading and the like."

Kathy looked down at Kira who was holding out her hand.

"Of course," Kathy took her hand. "We're going to help with the horses."

"That's grand, Kira loves horses."

"See you, Mary," Heath nodded walking ahead and mumbling that the woman was mad. Kathy and Kira followed him to the stables and saw Kieran, standing with his thumbs tucked under his braces. He nodded as they arrived.

"Alright Heath, Kathy." He looked nervously at Kira.

"He's uncomfortable 'round Kira. Worried the good people might take the horses if they upset her."

"Kira, why don't you collect some leaves?" Kathy asked.

Kira nodded and walked a few feet away from them, over to a tree. This seemed to satisfy Kieran, as he calmed down and handed Heath a brush. Kathy walked over to Rosie, the white horse and stroked her mane. Heath was busying himself brushing Rosie, when he looked up and dropped the horse's brush.

Heath cursed and bent down to pick it up. Kathy looked up as the group of girls from her caravan approached them, along with a boy she hadn't seen before. Kathy recognised Birgitta followed by Fallon and Moira.

"So, this is where you're keeping your new girlfriend," Birgitta chanted. She had her arms linked around a heavily built boy in a tight t-shirt.

Kathy rolled her eyes while the boy flexed his arm muscles.

"Do you think he likes her as much as he likes that horse, Moira?" Birgitta whispered, smirking and looking to the brunette on her left.

"Hi Birgitta," Heath mumbled, tapping the horse's brush onto his palm.

"Heath," the muscular boy said, reaching his hand out.

"Feck off," Heath spat at his feet.

"There's no need for that," the other boy continued in his deep voice.

"Yeah, you've clearly moved on," Moira said, throwing Kathy a dirty look.

Heath blushed and mumbled something derogatory under his breath. Kathy walked next to Heath. Birgitta was about to say something when Laoise emerged between two caravans next to the stables area. She walked over to Birgitta.

"Everything alright?" she asked, adjusting her black cape. Birgitta nodded stiffly, dropping the boy's arm. Heath was still eyeing the muscular boy, his arms tightly crossed over his chest. Laoise's eyes fell on Kathy, who looked up to briefly meet her gaze before looking down at her shoes. Without saying anything else, the old woman turned on her heel and strolled into the woods.

Birgitta walked over to where Laoise stood and picked up a very old silver key from the ground.

"Should I run back to her?" Heath asked.

"No," Birgitta backed away. "I've always wanted to see the inside of her caravan."

"Birgitta..."

"...All this time I've known her, she's never let me inside. She's always made me do lessons outside of the caravan. I have a right to know what's inside."

The muscular boy walked over and placed his hand on her waist. "I don't think that's a good idea."

"You're such a coward, Braden," she replied, shrugging him off.

Heath laughed. "Not so brave outside of the ring are we?"

"Watch it," Braden threatened, moving towards him.

"Are you volunteering to come with me?" Birgitta asked, looking up at Heath with doe-eyes.

"I'm done with your games," Heath replied.

She shrugged and looked at everyone else in the group. "Anyone?" Birgitta threw a dirty look at Moira who was occupying herself with her compact mirror and lipstick. Fallon was busy kicking some dirt with her shoes.

Kathy looked around and after a few seconds, she cleared her throat. "I'll come."

Birgitta looked down at her for a moment, failing to hide her disappointment. But, as it was her only option, she stifled a short nod.

"You don't need to do this Kath," Heath whispered.

"Don't listen to your boyfriend Kath, we're more fun," Birgitta smiled, placing her hands on her hips.

They decided to take different routes to Laoise's caravan to avoid any suspicion. Heath and Kira walked with Kathy to the fire. Kathy held back with Birgitta when they reached the old caravan. Heath walked past them and met Braden and Kieran. The three of them split up, Braden walked over to Paddy, while Kieran and Heath started to speak with Courtney and Bree to distract them. Kira and Moira moved to either side of the caravan to keep watch. After confirming everyone was in their positions, Birgitta nodded to Kathy. Quickly, they walked up to the orange door. Birgitta shoved Kathy to one side and inserted the silver key into the lock. It clicked instantly and the two girls slipped into the caravan, closing the door behind them.

"I can't see a fecking thing," Birgitta moaned. The inside of the caravan was completely dark, except for a small line of sunlight that crept through the drapes.

"Should we pull back the curtains?" Kathy asked, coughing at the stale, incensed air.

"Don't be daft," Birgitta hissed. "She doesn't even open them while she's in."

After a few minutes, their eyes adjusted to the darkness and they started to explore. Birgitta walked up to a table with a black cloth draped over it. Melted candles and illustrated cards scattered the surface of it. Kathy reached out to pick up a card but Birgitta quickly slapped her hand away.

"Don't touch them, it's bad luck," she whispered.

Kathy rubbed the back of her hand and walked away from the table. A soft whispering was coming from the bed across the room.

"Do you hear that?" Kathy asked, walking up to the bed. But the whispering had stopped.

"Hear what?" Birgitta snapped, opening up a jar on Loaise's shelf.

"It was over here," Kathy continued. She knelt down and removed a pile of quilts off of what looked like an old travelling chest.

"What do you think it is?" Kathy asked, stroking the top of it. She picked up the padlock. It looked old and rusted.

Birgitta sat down next to her. "It's locked," she said simply, looking over at Laoise's bedside table. She picked up a small vial and investigated the contents of it. Kathy reached behind Birgitta's head and removed a hairpin from her bun.

"Watch it!" Birgitta hissed, her hands quickly smoothing out the stray hairs.

"Move over," Kathy instructed. She picked up the padlock and inserted the hairpin. Kathy leaned her head closer to the lock and listened for a soft click.

"Hurry up!" Birgitta whispered, looking back at the door. Kathy moved the pin to the left and, with a final click, the padlock unlatched. Carefully, Kathy removed it from the chest and the two girls hauled the top open. It released a cloud of dust, inducing a coughing fit in both of them. Eagerly, they waved the dust from their faces.

Birgitta reached into the chest and picked up the

first item. "What is it?" she asked, turning it on either side.

"It's a book," Kathy said, grabbing it from Birgitta's hands. Kathy felt the smooth leather against her fingers. She wiped the dust off the title and read it aloud, "The Book of Moons."

"Jesus, I didn't think that actually existed," Birgitta said, stunned. "You should put it back. It's bad luck for anyone who isn't a storyteller to touch it."

Kathy ignored Birgitta's comment and flipped it open. She flicked through the dusty contents. It was too dark to read it inside the caravan but she could feel that the pages were old on the edges. She didn't know why, but holding the book in her hands felt comfortable.

A sharp knock on the door brought Kathy back into the room.

"Quick, we need to go!" Birgitta reached for the book to put it back into the chest.

Kathy moved it away from Birgitta's hands. "I'm keeping it."

"You can't! We shouldn't even see it; they only belong with storytellers! What if she notices it's gone?" Birgitta hissed.

"You saw the dust on this, she won't know it's missing," Kathy countered.

Birgitta looked at the door and back at Kathy. "Fine, but it's your funeral." She closed the chest and locked the padlock.

Kathy threw the quilts on top of the chest and they rushed to the door. Kathy hid the book behind her back while Birgitta opened the door an inch to peer outside. Heath, still speaking with Courtney near the fire, gestured behind his back for them to exit quickly. They scrambled out of the room, closing the door quietly behind them.

Kathy grabbed Birgitta's arm. "The key!" she hissed. Birgitta searched her skirt's pocket and found the key. She dropped it on the ground near the caravan's steps. They walked around the caravan and grinned widely, believing they had succeeded in sneaking into Laoise caravan. Until they bumped into Laoise, who was standing behind her trailer.

"Sorry," they both mumbled, looking down at their shoes and moving out of her way.

Laoise smiled before walking swiftly past them. They waited for her to walk around her caravan before running back to the horses.

They arrived just as the others got there. Both Birgitta and Kathy couldn't help but laugh and clutch at their ribs, gasping for air.

Heath rushed over to them both, his face blotched with red. "I hope you're happy. I've angered Courtney. I don't think I'll ever see another pudding again."

Kathy smiled widely and revealed the book from behind her back. "Look what we found!"

Heath reached out to hold the leather-bound book. Kathy placed it in his open palms. He turned it over and ran his finger down the gold embossed pages.

"Wow, I've never seen a story book before. I didn't think any of them existed anymore." Heath looked up with a mixture of awe and fear. "It's bad luck to have one if you're not a storyteller," Heath said nervously, handing the book back to Kathy.

"It's worse than that. It's The Book of Moons. I told her she should have left it there," Birgitta said.

Heath inhaled sharply. "I don't know if you want to be messing with that, Kath. There's been a lot of tales about Travellers trying to steal that book and never being seen again."

"But there are no more storytellers, you said so yourself," Kathy countered.

"Even so, that there's been blessed with fairy magic," Braden added. "They said the original storyteller was given The Book of Moons from the Finbeara."

Kathy looked over to Heath with a look of confusion on her face.

"He's the High King of the Daoine Sidhe, the good people," Heath explained. "It's said that the storyteller saved his people from a great war. In exchange, he gave him this book."

Kathy looked around the group. Everyone seemed uncomfortable and had taken a few steps away from the her. Except for Kira, who still stood close to Kathy. Kira looked up and smiled at her.

"But these are just stories. Of course storytellers are going to tell you this to keep their books safe."

"Maybe, but why chance it?" Heath asked.

***

Kathy kept the book near her at all times. She read it outside in the woods when she had the opportunity, or in the caravan on rainy days, while the others were out and Heath was practicing his fiddle. Birgitta made it clear that she didn't want it near her, so at night Kathy kept it hidden under her pillow. One evening, while Kathy sped through her supper, Heath confronted her.

"I know where you're going," he whispered. "It's like you're obsessed with that book."

Kathy pushed her plate away, wiping her mouth on her sleeve.

"I'm not obsessed, it's just really interesting."

"More interesting than my company?"

"We're with each other all day. Besides, you spend your evenings tinkering away on your fiddle."

"Fair enough. But shouldn't you be finding a talent? You haven't asked Cian yet to teach you how to carve. And you still need to try the fiddle."

"I will, later. I promise."

Kathy hurried back to the caravan. She walked over to the bed and grabbed the book from under her pillow, plopping it on her lap. The book was old and written in a fancy handwriting that made it difficult at times to read. There were inscriptions in the margins, making it even harder to understand.

Kathy managed to read a few pages before the door swung open. Kira walked in. Kathy patted the bed to signal that she could join her. Kira looked down at the book. Kathy handed it to her, and the little girl flipped through the pages.

"Would you like me to read it to you?" Kathy asked.

Kira smiled and nodded. She got herself under

the covers and closed her eyes. Kathy started to read from one of the earlier stories about children that were turned into swans by their evil stepmother. When she finished the story Kira was fast asleep. Her tiny chest was rising and falling. The sun had started to set making it difficult for Kathy to see. She stuffed the book under her pillow and closed her eyes. She listened to the sounds of Birgitta, Moira and Fallon drunkenly stumbling into the caravan. They were laughing at something and trying to keep their voices down. Kathy listened to Kira's breath and soon fell fast asleep.

***

The next day, Kathy asked Cian to show her how to carve wood. Kathy's clumsiness made it almost impossible to do anything, and she was left with a sore finger wrapped in cloth.

"What's wrong?" Heath asked, walking up to Kathy who was sitting next to the fire.

"Splinter," she replied gloomily, lifting her hand gently before throwing some sticks into the flames.

"Oh c'mon Kath, you haven't tried everything. I've brought my fiddle along, I thought we could see if there's a virtuoso in you."

Kathy rolled her eyes. "We can try but I'm not promising anything."

Kathy followed Heath into the woods near their camp and found a clearing with a log. He sat on top of it and patted the bit beside him for Kathy to take a seat.

"Right, so this is a bow and this is a fiddle," Heath explained, stretching out his arms so Kathy could see both parts in each hand.

Kathy rolled her eyes. "Let's skip the introduction and get to the point. I'm telling you, I'm going to be awful at this."

"You won't get anywhere with that attitude."

Kathy grabbed the fiddle from his hand and placed it on her shoulder, as she saw Heath do the other day.

"Good placement," he replied, smiling.

"Bring your right hand with the bow and move it gently on the strings. Excellent, now the left hand will press down on certain strings. The strings that you hold while moving the bow creates a note." Kathy nodded.

"So this," he said while moving the fingers on her left hand to cover two strings. "Is an F sharp."

Kathy tried to memorise which fingers were on what strings.

"Good, hold those strings, not too tight, and gently bring the bow down along the base."

Kathy brought the bow down on the strings but pressed too firmly and ended up slipping it along the base, making an awful sound.

Heath was very patient, and despite Kathy's consistent failure to grasp even the simplest concepts about the instrument, he kept encouraging her. It was only when their stomachs started to growl that they finally decided to call it a day.

"That wasn't so bad," Heath encouraged. "I mean for someone with no musical background, you did really well."

"I was awful," Kathy mumbled, slumping down next to Kieran who was picking hay from his hair.

Heath sat on the other side of Kathy, clearing his throat loudly to interrupt Birgitta and Braden who were preoccupied with kissing each other intensely.

"D'you mind? I have to eat on this fecking table," Heath said.

Courtney walked over with a tray of bowls, placing an Irish stew in front of everyone. Kathy gave her a big smile but Courtney rolled her eyes.

"Don't know why you try to be friendly with her, she doesn't like anyone," Heath explained, stuffing his mouth full of soup. Birgitta picked at the brown mush in front of her.

"So what were you two doing in the woods?" she teased.

"Mind your business," Heath spat, spewing pieces of food in her direction. Birgitta looked at him with disgust.

"Heath was trying to teach me to play the fiddle," Kathy explained, picking a piece of potato from her bowl and plopping it into her mouth.

"That's daft. If you're looking for a real talent you should do tarot."

"Is that what you do?" Kathy asked.

"I dabble in it."

"Don't sell yourself short Birgitta. You're the most talented girl in the camp," Braden said, squeezing her closer. Heath snorted into his bowl.

"Can you teach me?" Kathy asked.

Birgitta rolled her eyes, pushing the bowl of stew toward Braden who had just finished off his own.

"You can't teach someone tarot, you either have it or you don't."

"Is that right?" Heath asked sarcastically. "Then why do you visit Laoise every other afternoon? Just for a bit of tea?"

"To perfect my gift," she snapped.

Kathy elbowed Heath in the ribs and whispered, "I know you're just trying to help but I'm terrible at the fiddle so perhaps I should try something else?"

"Fine," he mumbled, digging into his stew.

"Perhaps you could introduce me to tarot? To see if I... er, have a gift for it?"

"I suppose I could tomorrow morning..."

"...and then we can show you a real talent in the afternoon," chanted Moira, while Fallon laughed.

Birgitta gave them a cold look and they turned their heads to giggle in silence.

"Okay, tomorrow."

Kathy finished the contents of her bowl quietly, avoiding eye contact with Heath.

"You know you're playing with fire."

"What do you mean?" she asked innocently, pushing her bowl away and pouring herself a cup of tea.

"They're not your friends. They'll only help you for as long as it's entertaining for them."

Kathy shrugged. "I know that but I really need to get to Dublin and maybe this tarot or palm reading thing might be something I can pick up quickly."

"They just can't be trusted Kathy." Heath leaned in and whispered in her ear, "What if they find out that you're not a Traveller?"

Kathy's stomach did a somersault. If any of the girls discovered Kathy's secret they would surely tell everyone. And would Laoise protect her again? Heath stood up and downed the last bit of tea from his mug before placing it sternly on the table.

"I'm going to bed," he mumbled, leaving Kathy and Kieran alone at the table.

"Do you think he's right?" Kathy asked Kieran, who was stirring his mug. He shook his head.

"They're not kind to him, those girls. And he took it pretty hard after he and Birgitta split up. They were with each other for two years before she cheated on him with Braden a few months back."

Kathy shook her head in disbelief. "He told me it was nothing serious."

"Oh they were serious. They were planning on setting up on their own. Getting a caravan and some horses. Heath's been saving since they've been together."

Kathy's heart dropped. He lied to her. She looked down at her mug of tea and swirled the contents.

"Do you think he's over her?" she asked quietly.

Kieran shrugged. "Not sure but she's sure over him," he stood up and stretched. "Girls are complicated, that's why I stay with the horses," he said, walking away and leaving Kathy to finish her tea.

***

The next morning, Kathy approached Birgitta about teaching her tarot. She shrugged and said, "Sure," while she tied the blue silk scarf into a bow on top of her head. They sat inside their caravan and listened to the rain beat against the wooden roof. Kira was on the bed, looking through her box of leaves. Moira and Fallon were on the top bunk whispering and giggling to one another as they looked down at their palms. Birgitta pulled out a deck of oversized cards from a silk bag. She split the deck and showed Kathy two cards.

"The deck has two parts. Major arcana," she explained, lifting the card that showed a wheel with illustrations around it. "And minor arcana," she picked up the second card that had a scene which looked like a wedding with two people holding cups.

"Within the minor arcana there are four suits: wands, pentacles, swords, and cups. The cups represent fertility and flow, the pentacles represent abundance in skills and materials, the swords represent strength and the wands represent power," Birgitta explained, showing Kathy a card from each suit.

"Understand?"

"So you just memorise the meaning of the cards and then tell people what they are?" Kathy asked.

Moira and Fallon looked up from their palm reading and laughed. Birgitta shot them an angry look.

"It's so much more than that. You need to really feel the cards and the person and their question. It's much more sophisticated than looking at some lines on a palm," she replied, giving Moira and Fallon a sharp look. They both went quiet and returned to their palm reading. "So what do the four minor arcana mean?" Birgitta asked.

"Er... I think wands are strength and pentacles mean fertility?" Kathy heard the sound of laughter from the corner of the caravan again.

Birgitta rolled her eyes and shook her head. She spent the rest of the morning explaining the meaning of different cards to Kathy. Afterwards, Birgitta tested Kathy but she only managed to remember the lovers and the two of cups. When lunchtime came around, they were both exhausted from a very unsuccessful attempt at learning tarot. Kathy felt self-conscious, she didn't realise it would be so difficult to find a talent.

After lunch, Kathy followed Moira and Fallon next to the fire. The rain had stopped and the sun was slowly drying the earth around them. Kathy held out her palm as Fallon and Moira pointed out the various lines that marked her hand. Fallon pointed at a visible line.

"See the long, top one? That's the head line. You read it from left to right."

"And the one below that, that's the heart line, you read it from right to left," Moira added, pointing to the one below it. Kathy squinted down at her palm.

"Okay, so this one is the heart line?"

Fallon ignored her question. "This one here will tell you about your travels. And this line will tell you about your career."

Moira stroked the thin line on Kathy's palm with her finger before saying, "And there's nothing here about being a palm reader." Fallon and Moira laughed at this. Kathy's cheeks blushed as she pulled her hand away.

"Ooh, did we upset you?" Fallon crooned mockingly, pouting her thin lips. She looked over at Moira and they fell into another fit of laughter. Kathy rolled her eyes and stood up from the log, cursing the two of them under her breath. She marched off with her arms crossed.

When Kathy returned to the caravan she found Kira outside on the steps looking at her box of leaves. Kathy approached and looked down at a flattened oak leaf.

"Would you like to go for a walk?" Kathy asked. Kira looked up and smiled. She placed the box next to her and took Kathy's hand. They left the spiral of caravans and walked along the edge of the trees.

"Shall we see the horses?" Kathy asked. Kira looked up at her with wide eyes.

"I don't believe what they say about you," Kathy said, reaching out to take Kira's hand and they walked to the other end of the camp where the horses were.

"Hey Kathy, wait up!" Kathy turned around. Moira was running up to join her.

"Oh hi," Kathy said, looking away.

"Listen, palm reading is hard. And I didn't really start until a few years ago. Before then I did some Irish dancing."

"Right," Kathy nodded and turned around again, headed to the horses.

"Wait... what I'm trying to say is that dancing

is loads easier, and maybe I could teach you some things?" Moira asked, a look of guilt spread across her tanned face. Kathy surveyed her green eyes before nodding shortly.

"Sure, that'd be nice."

"Grand, see you."

Kathy turned away and walked with Kira to the horses.

"Kieran isn't even here," Kathy said reassuringly, as they approached the white horse. "This one is named Rosie. Would you like to pet her?"

Kira nodded. Kathy bent down and picked her small body up so she could reach the horse. Her small hands stroked the white mane.

Kathy smiled. "I think she likes you." Kathy placed Kira down and walked over to a bucket with carrots. She picked one up and gave it to Kira.

"I read in a book once that you just hold it in front of the horse's mouth. It'll want to smell it first and then it will eat from your palm."

Kira stood completely calm while the white horse ate from her palm.

"Oi, Kathy, what are you doing?" asked a voice from behind. The horse, startled, backed away and huffed before turning around quickly and trotting into the woods. Kathy pulled Kira closer to her as Kieran ran up towards them with a bread roll in his hand.

"Ye frightened Rosie!" he called, turning to run into the woods after the horse. "Keep that fairy child away from here," he shouted back, before he was enveloped by the trees.

Kira's eyes started to water and her lower lip trembled.

"Oh Kira, I'm so sorry, I didn't mean for that to happen." Kathy bent down to give her a hug.

"Shall we find Mary?" Kathy asked. Kira nodded in response.

They walked through the camp and found Mary humming and sitting around the centre fire with a blanket laid across her knees. As they got closer, Kathy noticed a pile of beads on Mary's lap, which she was picking from before adding them to a string.

"Hello Kira, Kathy," she said as they approached.

"Would you like to help me make some jewellery?" she asked.

Kira opened her palm and Mary dropped a few beads into the hollow it made. She handed Kathy a small string.

"Just give it a knot at the end... there, that's it. Now drop a bead and knot it again."

Kathy did as she was instructed. Knotting each end of the string after picking a bead from Kira's hand. They did this together as they listened to Mary's humming before she looked up.

"So how are you liking the camp, Kathy?"

Kathy smiled. "It's nice, I'm just struggling to find a talent. Something so they'll let me stay."

Mary nodded and said darkly, "Yes, talents are important here and the like. It's a wonder they never threw me out when I couldn't sing no more."

"But you have such a beautiful voice, like the way you hum that song. I'm sure you can sing if you tried."

Mary lowered her hands to her lap and looked into the fire. "I do, but every time I open my mouth to sing, the only thing that comes out is my humming to that song."

Kathy tied another bead onto her string. "Heath said it was because of the good people?" Kathy asked, looking down at her half-finished bracelet.

Mary nodded and was about to speak but Kieran and another man with shaggy, blonde hair stormed up to them.

"You see here Mary, you need to keep that girl away from our horses," the man said, pointing down at Kira.

Mary looked up with her dark eyes. "I don't know what you mean, Tommy," she replied simply, returning back to her bracelet.

"Kira here scared Rosie all the way to the river. She's gone and hurt her hoof now," Tommy replied.

"Kira had no intention of hurting any of them horses," Mary snapped. "You leave your superstitions to yourself, Tommy. Don't be bringing it around the child." Mary wrapped her arm around Kira and pulled her in closer.

Kira buried her head against Mary's red dress. Tommy's cheeks blushed. He turned on his heel and walked away without saying another word. Kieran stood there and looked down at Kathy.

"You know better than that Kathy. Every Traveller knows to keep changelings away from the horses." He walked away shaking his head. Kathy looked over to Kira, who was shaking and crying.

"I'm sorry Mary, it's my fault. I wanted her to see the horses."

Mary rocked the child in her arms, humming her song. Angry tears poured down her cheeks. She shook her head. "This is nothing to do with you. It's them and their superstitions. Nothing but ridiculous stories these men tell themselves and the like," She hummed some more, burying her face into Kira's hair as the child shook with tears.

Kathy lowered her hands to her lap. She placed the unfinished bracelet next to them on the bench and stood up. She hurried away from the fire, tears stinging her cheeks from embarrassment.

Kathy found Heath sitting at the table, tuning his fiddle. She slumped herself down and buried her head in her arms.

"Bad day?" he asked, plucking a few notes.

"I'm desperate, Heath. I just want to get to Dublin but I've got less than a week left to find a talent if I'm going to get there." He lowered his fiddle on the table.

"It'll be alright Kath, you'll find something."

"You don't know that. Why do you even care if I stay?" Kathy stood up from the table.

Heath's ears started to turn pink. "I just want to see you get to your friend, that's all."

"You're not helping."

"At least I'm trying, all you do is spend your time reading that book of yours. Or you're with Kira and Mary all the time. You're not exactly helping yourself, are you?"

"It's not like you're around." Kathy looked down

at his fiddle. "You gave me one lesson and then gave up on me. Guess I'm not worth much of your time." She turned and walked back into the camp to the large fire. She threw herself angrily on the ground and dug her nails into the dirt. She squeezed it into her fists until her knuckles turned white.

"I find it therapeutic too," a voice said. Kathy turned around and found Laoise standing behind her. "Touching the ground." She nodded at Kathy's hands which were still clutching dirt. Kathy released her fist and felt the blood rush back into her fingers. She wiped her hands on her skirt.

"I'm sorry," Kathy mumbled, wiping her cheeks with her palm. "I'm trying to find a talent and it's not going so well," Kathy said, looking down at her Oxford shoes. They were shiny when Kathy first arrived but had now collected scratches and a thick covering of mud under her soles.

"Why don't you come in for a cup of tea?" Laoise asked, gesturing to her caravan. Kathy looked around and shrugged. She stood up and followed the old woman into her caravan.

It was strange to be inside again, knowing she had broken in with Birgitta just over a week ago. Oddly, this time the curtains on the windows were pulled back, letting the sunlight pour over the old furniture. A large oak table sat on one end with cards strewn across it. Laoise walked over to the cast-iron stove and placed a tin kettle on top of it. She gestured for Kathy to take a seat at the table. Kathy stared at the different images on the cards. She was about to reach out and pick one up when Laoise placed a mug in front of her. "Sugar?" she asked. Kathy looked up startled and nodded awkwardly. Laoise reached over and grabbed a small china bowl with sugar cubes in it. Kathy looked down at the table around her.

"How are you suppose to read these if they don't have any words on them?" Kathy sighed, picking one up and turning it over. It was the card with two cups on the front Birgitta taught her about, which Kathy forgot the meaning of.

Laoise walked over to the table and took a seat across from Kathy. "Biscuit?" she asked, moving the tin closer to her. Kathy nodded and took a shortbread biscuit from the tin.

"You don't read them in the usual sense," Laosie answered. "You come to understand them and their meanings by the symbols on the cards," Laoise explained, picking a card that had a naked woman pouring water from a jug into a river, with bright stars above her.

"Each card is illustrated with symbols. A bit like words really. And they all add up to create a story." She handed the card to Kathy. Kathy accepted it and inspected it further.

"Why are they laid out like that?"

"It's a spread. One of the oldest and most popular. It's called the Celtic Cross." Kathy instinctively reached for her own cross around her neck and felt the points press into her fingers.

Laoise walked back to the stove and poured the boiling water into a teapot. They sat in silence as

Kathy looked down at the cards on the table. Laoise poured some steeped tea into their cups.

"Why did you let me stay?" Kathy asked quietly, dropping two sugar cubes into her mug and bringing it to her lips.

"I don't believe in coincidences Kathy. I think you're here for a reason. And I wouldn't let the fact that you weren't born here to get in the way of that."

Kathy lowered her mug. "So you know I'm not a Traveller then?"

Laoise shook her head. "I know you didn't come from another Traveller clan. But that doesn't mean you're not a Traveller."

"It doesn't?"

Laoise removed her spectacles and rubbed her tired eyes with her ringed hand before placing them back on her long, thin nose. "You can be whatever you like. It's a choice whether you want to be an Irish Traveller or not."

Kathy nodded and finished the last drop of tea in her mug. Laoise picked up the cards and shuffled them into a pile. Kathy looked out of the window and saw Birgitta staring back at her on the other side. She opened her mouth to say something but Birgitta turned on her heels and ran off.

"I... I need to go," Kathy said, setting the cup down on the table. Laoise nodded and coughed into a handkerchief.

"Good luck." Kathy looked back. "On finding the talent."

"Thanks."

Kathy walked around the caravan to where she saw Birgitta standing outside the window. But Birgitta had already started to run across the camp towards their own caravan. Kathy jogged across the camp and found Birgitta standing outside their door. She was pacing back and forth, her hands on her hips. Tentatively, Kathy walked up to her.

"It's not what you think," Kathy explained.

"I know what you're doing," she hissed back.

"I didn't know she was going to invite me in."

"At least now I know why you wanted to learn tarot so badly," Birgitta said, running her fingers angrily through her blonde hair. "If anyone is in line to replace that old woman it's me." She jabbed a thin finger into Kathy's chest. Kathy felt it sting and backed away.

"I'm not trying to replace anyone. I just want to get to Dublin."

Birgitta threw back her head and laughed mockingly. "Like I believe that! What's in Dublin then? If you need to get to it?"

"I just do."

Birgitta rolled her eyes. "I'm not going to buy your lies like Heath, and I'm not going to let you get in my way." Birgitta turned around and walked into their caravan, slamming the door behind her.

Chapter Five

An Old Talent

As the end of the month drew closer to the Midnight Circus, Kathy spent less time trying new things and more time reading. The tension between Kathy and Heath hadn't subsided. One afternoon, while Kathy was sitting in the woods, Heath walked up to her, his hands in his pocket.

"What are you still doing with that book, Kath?" he asked, shaking his head.

Kathy looked up from the book and closed the cover. Tilting her head next to the oak tree she was sitting against she replied sharply, "This isn't the one from Laoise's caravan."

Heath shook his head and sat cross legged next to her. Sheepishly, he reached out his arm to place his hand on her shoulder. "I didn't mean to upset you. It just... unsettles me, that's all. We don't normally have books around here."

"You don't have books here?"

"Travellers don't know how to read. We don't really have a need for it. Except if you're a storyteller then I s'pose you need to learn the stories from somewhere."

"Is that a talent then?" she asked, running her finger down the spine of the book.

"Storyteller? Course it is. We haven't had one in fifty years. Doubt we'll ever get one again. Laoise says they've gone extinct."

"Maybe I could be a storyteller."

Heath laughed and looked up at her. "No offence Kath but that's not just something you become. Storytellers are like Gods to us, you know. It's something you're just born into." Kathy threw her book on the ground and stood up abruptly.

"So you don't think I'm good enough then, is that it?"

Heath looked up confused. "No Kath, that's not what I mean. It's just that they're really rare, that's all."

"I suppose you prefer tarot readers anyway, don't you?" Kathy spat as she turned on her heels and stormed into the woods. She felt her chest heave with rage as she chewed on her lip. She was angry with him. Didn't he want her to stay? How could he say she wasn't good enough to be a storyteller? Kathy shook her head and lent against a tree. She rested her forehead against its bark and drew in a long breath. Angry tears started to sting her eyes. Closing them didn't bring any relief. All she could picture was Heath with Birgitta. His muscular arms wrapped around the curves of her body. His hands stroking her long blonde hair. She closed her eyes tightly and tried to rid the image from her mind.

"Kath, wait up!" Heath shouted, catching up to her. When he reached the tree she was leaning against he bent forward to catch his breath.

"You dropped your book," he said sheepishly, looking up with his green eyes. Kathy took the paperback book that was now wet around the edges.

"Kieran told me you were with Birgitta for two years," Kathy said, not looking at him.

Heath walked around the tree to look her in the eyes. "She doesn't mean anything to me anymore."

"Then why didn't you tell me the truth? You made it out like it didn't matter. But it did. He said you two were going to run off together," Kathy said, her stomach tightened.

"What about you, Kath? What's the plan when you get to Dublin. You're just gonna run off with your friend and then what?"

"No," she whispered softly, tears running down her cheeks. "But you obviously still love Birgitta. I see the way you look at her. And the way you get so angry at Braden."

"I don't love her." He grabbed Kathy's shoulders with both hands and stared intently into her eyes. She looked away. "Look at me Kathy... I've never met anyone like you before. How can I even look at Birgitta when you're near me? You're like, like a breath of fresh air. You're special. You say you haven't seen the world but when I look into those eyes I can see a thousand places that I'll never be able to see. You're incredible Kath and I want to be with you."

He pressed his soft lips against hers and Kathy felt her stomach somersault into a sweet surrender. He wrapped his arms around her waist and pulled her body close. Kathy felt the firmness of his stomach against her own and the weight of his arms wrapped tightly around her. Many times she had thought about what her first kiss might be like. She always believed she might do something wrong. Would she know what to do? Sinead and her would stay up at night and giggle about it together. But now, Kathy knew everything she needed to know. She threaded her fingers through his curly hair and moved in rhythm with his mouth. Her cheeks burned with pleasure; his kisses tasted sweet like honey and morning dew. When they pulled apart, breathless, she couldn't help but laugh. Heath look stunned and combed his fingers through his hair. She brought her hand to her mouth.

"I'm like a breath of fresh air?"

"Oh do shut up," he pulled her in closer and their lips met again in a beautiful tandem. She felt rain against her hot skin, which sent a cool shiver down her spine. She wanted more than just this, something inside her awoke and these kisses weren't quenching it. Kathy pulled back and placed her hand above her head to try to shelter her hair from the rain but it made no difference. They were completely soaked.

"Oh no," Kathy dropped down and picked up the book that fell earlier. It was completely wet. "My book!" she cried.

Heath wrapped his arms around her. "C'mon, let's dry it in your caravan."

They ran through the woods together and back to the warm caravan. When they arrived, they barged through the door, laughing and knocking some wellies to the side. When they approached the small stove, Heath opened the door and threw a few logs onto the cinders. It caught quickly and the flames grew. Kathy shook the book gently.

"Here, let's hang it on this line." Heath removed the stockings and socks from the laundry line and gently laid them onto the table. He took the book from Kathy and carefully placed it on the line above the stove. "It looks old," he said, examining the front cover with its bent corners.

"I've had it for a long time," Kathy replied, wringing her wet hair with her hands. Heath waited for her to explain but she remained silent. He looked into the fire as it flickered brightly. He stretched his hands forward to warm his palms.

"I never met either of my parents, you know. My ma' died in childbirth, of a broken heart they say. My da' died a few days earlier in a horse accident. Threw him off and he just didn't wake up after that." Kathy leaned forward to touch his shoulder.

"I'm sorry Heath," she whispered. He looked down at his wrist and played with the leather bracelet.

"Don't worry about it. Cian and Sloane have been like parents all the while. He made this for me, you know." He gestured to his bracelet.

"Made it after my first performance. I did so poorly, I threw up and everything. Couldn't even remember the second half of the set. But he gave it to me and said he was proud of me. Not because I did well, but because I did it at all. He said that's the true mark of a man, if he can go up and try, even without knowing what will happen." Heath smiled at his wrist and looked over to Kathy.

"I think you're incredibly brave too, Kath. I know

it wasn't easy leaving that place in Ennis but you had faith that you'd make it. That both you and Sinead would escape." Kathy nodded, watching the wood burn.

"You'll see her again Kath, I have a good feeling about it."

***

Kathy woke the next morning to the smell of coffee beans roasting. She turned to her side and opened her sleepy eyes. A mass of black hair was sprawled on the pillow next to her. There was something cosy about Kira's presence. She looked up at the beautiful stained glass windows on either side of the wagon. The dewy smell in the air was now mixed with the scent of an open fire and she smiled. There was comfort in these smells and sights.

Kathy suddenly felt her stomach drop and her mind flashed to Sinead. She was still nowhere closer to Dublin and without a talent, she would soon have to find her own way there. Heath seemed convinced they would discover something for Kathy but she was beginning to feel less hopeful each day. Kathy crept from her bed, while the others continued to sleep. She quietly pulled on her black, wool dress and stockings before stepping out of the warm room.

The sun was still rising and only a few people were moving about. Kathy could hear people stirring in their caravans as she walked past them. The fire in the centre of the camp was slowly building its girth. Bree and Courtney were shuffling around, stacking washed dishes from the night before. Cian was huddled over the small flame, holding what looked like a frying pan with a very long handle.

"Mornin'," he said, shaking the pan.

"Morning," Kathy replied.

"Smell that?" Cian asked. Kathy nodded and kneeled next to him.

"Freshly roasted coffee beans," he explained, shaking the pan again.

She smiled. The green beans were starting to turn into an earthy brown colour.

"Heath's taken a liking to you," he said, his eyes focussed on his roasting pan.

"I guess." Kathy nodded nervously

"He's a good lad right enough though he can get himself into trouble but he's a good Traveller. He's got a lot going for him too in the community," Cian explained nodding at the fire. "Talented fiddler if I ever saw one, even better than Paddy O'Sullivan but if you tell him that, I'll deny it." Cian winked. He cleared his throat before continuing. "I guess what I mean to say is that Heath is a Traveller and he's meant for a Traveller girl. And though Laoise has calmed Sloane's thinkings that yer not a Traveller at this moment, I can't see that lastin' very long," he sighed, giving the beans a quick shake before leaning back. "We have our own customs and ways you see. Heath is young and reckless but when he gets older he's gonna need a good companion that can share those customs and ways with him."

Kathy looked down at her hands, still pale and

smooth compared to the others in the camp. "I see," she said quietly.

"Now, I know you haven't been able to find a talent and like we agreed we're going to drop you off in Athlone, the next town after our Midnight Circus. So I'm asking you, Kathy, to leave our young Heath with us. Don't be encouraging him to come with you." Cian looked up to her, pleading. "We're just not ready to see him go and we'll never forgive ourselves if we knew he wasn't with his own kind."

Kathy stood abruptly, anger swelled in her chest. "I can't make any promises; that's up to Heath."

Cian pulled the roasting pan off the fire and onto the ground. He looked up at Kathy and said softly, "I mean ye no harm, I just want you to think what's best for our young Heath. I know ye care for him and all. But you've got your own way to go and that's a separate way from our boy."

Kathy turned on her heels before she could listen to anymore of his cruel words. She felt a wave of anger creep up from her stomach. She rushed through the spiral of caravans, not wanting anyone to see her tears.

"Kathy!" Mary called from the steps of her bright green caravan, with a sleepy Kira on her lap. "Everything okay?"

Kathy turned, unclenched her fists and walked up to them. Kira jumped down from Mary's knee and gave Kathy a hug.

"Sorry, I'm just upset that I'll be leaving soon," Kathy said, stroking Kira's hair.

"Oh child, that is a sad thing. But don't you worry,

the people who come here always find a way of staying and the like."

Kathy gave her a small smile and nodded. Kira took her hand and pulled her over to the stairs.

"I think Kira wants to show you what she's made," Mary explained, lifting up a small beaded bracelet. "We were going to keep it as a farewell gift but I guess Kira here believes you won't be leaving us very soon after all."

Kira lifted Kathy's arm for Mary, who wrapped the small beaded bracelet around Kathy's wrist and tied the ends tightly together. Kathy looked at it closely. She had placed purple and red beads between a beautiful criss-crossed pattern.

"It's the trinity knot," Mary explained, nodding at the bracelet. She lifted Kira onto her lap. "It means eternity." She brushed Kira's hair. "The beginnings are the endings to our beginnings and the like," she explained before humming quietly to herself.

"Thanks Kira," Kathy said, touching the small beads. Kira looked up at her and smiled with bright eyes.

"You should run along to Courtney now, she's looking for help to collect mushrooms for tonight's soup." Kathy nodded and headed back to the direction of the large fire. Cian was now gone and coffee had been handed out to everyone. Bree was carrying a stack of dirty mugs to a basin filled with soapy water. Kathy spotted Heath standing next to Braden and Birgitta, who were holding hands. Moira and Fallon hovered over something Courtney was showing them.

"Morning," Heath said brightly as she walked toward him. "I went to your caravan and you weren't there."

Kathy looked down at her bracelet. "I woke up early. I've just been chatting to Mary and Kira." She wanted to mention the conversation she had with Cian but there were too many people around.

"What's everyone looking at?" Kathy asked, standing on her toes so she can see past Braden's shoulders.

"Courtney's laying out some mushrooms. She wants us to earn our supper, she says."

"Does anyone else smell manure?" snarled Birgitta as Kieran joined the group.

"Watch it Birgitta," Heath hissed from the corner of his mouth.

"Shush, the lot of you," Courtney snapped, standing up and wiping her hands on her apron. "I've got better things to do than listen to your nonsense."

Moira and Fallon fell into a fit of giggles.

Courtney shot them a nasty look which silenced them immediately.

"I need mushrooms for our soup tonight and you are all going to forage for me. Now, you're going to look for these two types of mushrooms." She held one that was about the size of tennis ball. "This is a giant puffball. They can come in bigger sizes too."

"Like in my pants," whispered Braden.

"Shut it," Birgitta muttered, elbowing him in the ribs.

"The second," Courtney growled. "Is a field

mushroom that looks like this." She held up a smaller, white mushroom with a perfectly rounded top.

"You should have no problem finding these," she said shortly. Courtney bent forward and dug through her basket. She removed another mushroom that looked identical to the field mushroom.

"However, this one looks just like the last but can give you a horrendous stomach pain that'll make you wish you were never born. So don't pick it. Understood?" She waved it around their faces and they instinctively took a step back.

Fallon raised her hand. "How do you know which is which?"

Birgitta rolled her eyes. "Isn't it obvious?"

Courtney ignored Birgitta's comment and explained, "Because of its smell and it'll turn yellow if it's bruised but don't ye be bruising my mushrooms to test them! Use your noses," she added sharply. They all nodded in reply.

"Right," she continued, dusting the dirt from her hands. "Pair up and collect some mushrooms, whoever gets the largest puffball gets extra pudding. And don't come back until you have at least a basket full each," she added, looking up at Bree. "Oi Bree, watch where you put that pot!" she shouted, shoving past the group and storming over to the clueless woman.

"C'mon, Kieran knows his way around these woods," Heath whispered, nudging Kathy away from Birgitta and Braden who started to snog, while Fallon and Moira fought over the smaller basket.

Heath patted Kieran's shoulder. "Kieran here is an

expert on this forest now. He sees wild mushrooms all the time when he takes the horses out. And he knows that there's nothing up their end but a dried-up stream. This path here leads to the river," Heath said, watching the other group move in the opposite direction to them.

Sure enough, Kieran's knowledge had proven to be fruitful. The three of them had filled their baskets full of field mushrooms and even a few giant puffballs. Of course, nobody's puffball was quite as glorious as Heath's. His was at least the size of a football, which he proudly repeated to Kathy and Kieran every few minutes.

To Kathy's delight, the others were not so victorious in their search. Their baskets were barely half full. When Heath, Kathy and Kieran returned, Courtney was scolding Fallon and Moira for having filled the bottom of their baskets with rocks.

"I thought I said I wanted a full basket. This is barely enough for a stew!" she shouted, snatching the baskets from both girls.

"And what is this one?" Courtney cried, reaching into Braden's basket.

"Didn't I say not to pick this?" she asked, shaking the mushroom in his face. Braden looked awkwardly at his feet. Courtney opened her mouth to scold him some more but her eyes flickered back to the mushroom. She brought her hand to her mouth as she investigated the yellow stains.

Heath leaned forward to get a better look at the mushroom. He looked back at Kathy and whispered,

"I think she sees something in the stain." Kathy leaned in and tried to get a glimpse of the mushroom Courtney was now rotating in her hand as she whispered under her breath.

"What is it?" Kathy asked.

"I don't know, but it doesn't look good."

"It's the fairy mark," Birgitta replied anxiously. "We need to put it back, right away. Exactly where we found it," she added hurriedly, her eyes wide with fear.

"I'll get Laoise," Birgitta said to Courtney, who acknowledged this with a short nod. Birgitta ran to the other side of the fire and knocked gently on the old caravan.

Laoise opened the door and after a few words were exchanged, the old woman marched quickly over to Courtney. Kathy watched as Courtney whispered something into Laoise's ear. She nodded and took the mushroom herself. Laoise looked at Birgitta through her turquoise spectacles.

"You know where you found this?" Laoise asked.

Birgitta nodded.

"Lead the way, Courtney, you know what to bring?"

Courtney nodded and hurriedly walked to the crate of kitchen items. Birgitta and Laoise walked through the camp. Courtney grabbed a tin of salt before looking up to face them all.

"Right, that's enough from you lot. Get out of my sight!" she snapped, pushing through the group and walking quickly to catch up with Birgitta and Laoise. Courtney disappeared into the woods with the two other women by her side. Bree tentatively approached them and started to collect their baskets in her feeble arms. She smiled sheepishly at Kathy when she reached her hand out to grab Kathy's basket.

"What will they do with it?" Kathy asked, whispering into Heath's ear as she handed her basket to Bree.

Heath scratched his head. "Laoise said we've only ever had this happen once before in our camp. Years back, when she was young. A fairy mark is a rare thing. They'll be bringing it back to the very bit of ground they picked it from. And then they'll need to make a ring of salt. I s'pose there'll be some words they have to say for good measure."

"But what does it mean?"

Heath swallowed and looked away before answering. "Death."

***

No one spoke of the fairy mark again that day. But its omen hung over the camp like a thick layer of fog, making everyone distressed and quiet. Kathy pushed it from her mind. She knew she had more urgent things to think about, like how she was getting to Dublin and her confrontation with Cian that morning. Kathy waited for an opportunity to tell Heath what Cian had said to her. While Kathy picked at the mushrooms in her soup, she waited for Kieran to finally finish his supper and return to the horses. Heath tipped his bowl back and finished the rest of his soup. He wiped his mouth on his sleeve and looked up at Kathy.

"Everything alright Kath? You barely touched yours."

Kathy shrugged her shoulders. "I spoke with Cian this morning, before I saw Mary and Kira."

Heath set his bowl down.

"It was just, he said that he thinks you deserve to be with a Traveller and he's worried that you're going to run off with me, when they drop me in a town. But it doesn't matter. I know you want to go to that horse fair and everything."

Heath leaned in closer and grabbed her hand. "I'm not going to that fair Kath. I'm going with you. I'll get you to Dublin."

Kathy looked up at him and replied, "What do you mean? What about the horse you want to buy?"

Heath looked around before leaning in and whispering, "I was going to tell you this later but I made a deal with Kieran. You know Rosie? Her hoof is not so good after she ran off into the woods that day Kira scared her. And anyway, I made a deal with him to buy her and he's agreed, since she won't sell at the fair now."

"But what about Cian and Sloane? What about everyone else here? I can't ask you to just leave everything and come with me."

"You're not asking Kath, I'm volunteering. Besides, I have my own dreams. Being a Traveller is great and all but I want to be more than just a travelling fiddler. I want to be the first Irish Traveller to make it as a professional fiddler and I can't do that here." He gestured around the camp. "That is, if you'll have me?" he asked with a crooked smile. He reached out his hand for hers. Kathy's stomach somersaulted.

She felt her cheeks blush. "Of course." She reached out her hand to meet his. She smiled softly as his rough skin met her own.

"So, it's a plan then," she said. "We're traveling to Dublin together?"

He gave her quick wink. "We're going solo."

***

Kathy and Heath made a plan to leave the clan of Travellers once they reached Athlone. They agreed to keep it a secret, for fear that Sloane and Cian might intervene. Apart from Keiran, no one else knew that Rosie belonged to Kathy and Heath.

The day before the Midnight Circus, Kathy sat next to the large fire. She was cupping her second serving of coffee and thinking about her and Heath's future journey together to Dublin. She wondered what it would be like when they were alone. And would they be able to make it all the way to Dublin?

Heath claimed he had some money saved, even after purchasing Rosie. And perhaps Kathy could make a few pence herself at the Midnight Circus, selling jewellery with Mary and Kira. As Kathy pondered these things, Moira approached her. Kathy looked up from her cup, startled and said, "Morning."

"Hi," Moira replied shortly. She stood in front of Kathy with her left hand on her hip, waiting. Her long, jet black hair pulled over one shoulder.

"Can I help?" Kathy asked, tipping the last few

dregs of coffee from her mug onto the ground.

"I'm supposed to teach you how to dance?" she answered impatiently, shifting her weight to the next hip.

"Oh right, of course," Kathy stood up and wiped the dirt from the front of her pleated skirt. "I forgot, sorry."

"I thought you said you wanted to stay."

Kathy blushed. "Yeah of course, I'd like to stay if I can."

"Let's see if you can pick up a few moves for tomorrow night." Moira turned and Kathy followed her to the edge of the camp.

"Do you have any training in Irish dancing?" she asked, kicking rocks away from the clearing to give them a better surface to work with. Kathy shook her head and replied, "No."

"You'll be fine. It's easy when you get the hang of it."

Unfortunately, it wasn't as easy as Moira said it would be. Kathy kept forgetting the steps and she even trotted on Moira's toes a few times. Moira was showing Kathy how to do a light jig for the third time when Sloane approached them between two caravans.

"Moira!" she called out. "What are you doing here?" she asked, grabbing Moira's wrist and pulling her away from Kathy. "You shouldn't be wasting your time with her, she's leaving tomorrow aren't you, Kathy?" Sloane asked sharply.

"Moira was just trying to teach me how to dance," Kathy replied, dumbfounded. Sloane dropped Moira's wrist and approached Kathy. Moira walked away with her arms crossed over her stomach.

"I don't care what Laoise might say about you." Sloane leaned in closer as she spoke. "I know you're not a Traveller. You stay away from my Heath, you here? I don't want you poisoning our boy with your ways," Sloane hissed, looking Kathy up and down. She turned away sharply and walked off before Kathy could say anything in return.

Kathy bent over, her heart pounding against her chest. She tried taking in deeper breaths but each time it was cut off with a sharp pain. Her stomach was sick. She felt embarrassed and scared. Sloane looked like she would do anything to keep Kathy away from Heath. What would happen if she found out they were leaving together tomorrow? Kathy covered her face with her hands. They'd make it, regardless of what she might think, they would leave the day after tomorrow and there was nothing Sloane could do about it.

Kathy spent the rest of the morning in the woods, away from the camp so she didn't have to interact with anyone. At lunch, Kathy made her way back to the large fire where she found Heath next to it, sitting on a rock. He was wrapping a few of his fingers in cloth. It was only when Kathy sat next to him that she noticed the cloth was drenched in a sappy substance. His exposed fingers were calloused and bleeding.

"What happened to your fingers?" Kathy asked, shocked.

"Oh this is normal. It happens when I play too much," Heath said. "It's nothing Kath, it's just these new numbers are quite complicated and they take a lot of practice," he added.

"You don't need to do this, we're going to be leaving after the circus," she whispered.

Heath shook his head. "It's not just about the Midnight Circus Kath, I want to be good enough for Dublin." Heath covered the last bit of his bleeding skin and tucked the end of the cloth underneath itself. "I'll be up against people who've been educated in this sort of stuff. They've learned to read music and everything." Heath picked up his bowl of stew and jabbed his spoon into it. "They're gonna think me a fool for showing up with nothing but some silly Traveller songs and an old fiddle."

Kathy put her arm around his shoulders. "That's not true, you're incredibly talented. Anyone can learn to read music but not everyone can feel it like you do."

Heath ran his hand through his hair and thought about this. "Maybe you're right."

"At least you know what you want. I just want to get to Dublin to find Sinead but after that I don't know what I'll do."

"But you went to school didn't you? Wasn't there something you enjoyed?"

Kathy picked at the pieces of her stew. "The only thing I really liked was reading. The orphanage had a very small library with all the classics. Sister Mary would let me borrow one each week. But reading isn't really a talent, is it?"

Heath looked down at his hand. "No, I suppose it isn't." He leaned in next to her, his head close to hers.

"But telling those stories is," he said, looking around to ensure no one else was listening.

"I thought you said that storytellers are like Gods and you can't just become one?"

"That's still true, but the settlers don't need to know that."

"I don't know if I'm any good," Kathy replied, looking down at her hands. They were pale compared to Heath's. Even after a month with the Travellers she still looked like an outsider.

"But you have that book don't you? That's all you need to learn those stories. When we're in Dublin it won't matter if you're not really a Traveller, people will want to hear them anyway. You won't find stories like that anywhere else and no other Traveller can read them like you can."

"I guess I could be a storyteller," Kathy said shyly, looking up with a smile.

Heath beamed, his eyes bright. "You're gonna be great Kath."

Chapter Six
The Midnight Circus

The day of the Midnight Circus was absolute chaos. Not only was everyone preparing and practicing for the night's event but they were also preparing everything for traveling immediately after the circus. Kathy did her part by trying her best to keep out of everyone's way. Somehow, that proved difficult; no matter where Kathy went, she was always bumping into people like Courtney, who almost toppled over her stack of buns that were to be sold that evening. More than a few times she had to jump out of the way as a horse came trotting toward her with Kieran panting shortly behind, stuttering an apology. After lunch, Kathy decided to take refuge in the forest. Mary had only asked her and Kira to come by her caravan after supper.

It was a bright sunny day. The sunlight poured through the trees and lit up the forest floor with hues of yellow and green. Kathy found the river where they gathered their water from each day and sat on the edge of it with her back against a large oak tree. She closed her eyes and listened to the sounds around her. The soft rustle of leaves and the birds chirping above. From a distance, she could make out what sounded like music. Kathy stood, wanting to hear more; she followed the notes as they echoed through the forest.

A few feet up the river she recognised Heath's

silhouette, leaning against a large tree. With his eyes closed, he rhythmically moved the bow along the fiddle's strings. He looked like he was in a trance, and his expression was so peaceful Kathy didn't want to disturb him. She turned to walk away quietly. But as she moved, she stepped on a fallen branch, snapping it in half. The music stopped and the last note hung on the air, waiting for a partner that would never come.

"I don't usually get an audience here," Heath said pleasantly.

"Sorry, I was just up the river when I heard you playing."

Heath nodded looking down at his fiddle. "I heard it last night in a dream. I came out here to try and remember it."

"It's beautiful," Kathy said, as she walked over to sit next to Heath. Heath crossed his arms and leaned back against the tree.

"S'pose it is. It's about saying goodbye to the places you know."

"You're going to miss them, aren't you?"

"Ay, I will. But sometimes you need to let go of the people that are no longer part of your story. I'm meant for another path. I need to take it, no matter how hard it might be."

Kathy folded her arms around her knees and rested her cheek against them. "Sloane approached me the other day. I think she knows I'm not a Traveller," Kathy explained with a sigh.

Heath dropped his fiddle on the ground and tightened his fists. "You should've told me Kath. It's none of their business who I spend my time with. They shouldn't be intimidating you like that."

Kathy nodded, and looked down, her auburn hair slipping onto her face from behind her ears. "But I know what it's like to be away from the people you love. I think they just want the best for you."

Heath leaned back against the tree and closed his eyes. He exhaled slowly before speaking again.

"When I found Birgitta with Braden in a caravan, almost naked, I couldn't take it so I ran to the river, just outside our camp, like this one here. I don't know what I was thinking but I took off my clothes, like I was possessed. I started to walk into the river. It was February, and the cold water pierced my skin in every part of my body. It was so painful but I couldn't stop myself. I just kept on walking to the centre where the currents started to pick up. I could hear people shouting from the riverbed. And then all I can remember is being forced back by Cian and Paddy. They dragged me from that river kicking and screaming. They said I was being possessed by themselves, that I had to wake up. That Tír na nÓg wasn't a place for me or my broken heart. Laoise came out with a tin of salt and started to throw it into the air chanting old Shanta." Heath rubbed his eyes and looked up at the tops of the trees. A light rain started to patter against the leaves.

"They think I was touched by the good people then, and they're afraid that I'm still not better. They think I'm making another reckless decision by being with you."

"Are you being reckless?"

"To be with a settled person? Ay, no doubt. That's not a normal Traveller thing to do, you see. But the thing is, I don't really want to be a normal Irish Traveller and I suspect that you're not a normal settler either."

Kathy looked down at her uniform from the orphanage. The four weeks of wear without washing had begun to show. Her skirt was covered with dirt and her white shirt was now a grey brown with a tinge of yellow under her arms. Her stockings had holes in them but Kathy continued to wear them because she was embarrassed by her naked legs. Kathy shook her head.

"No, definitely not normal." She smoothed the front of her skirt and watched the rain drops darken the fabric. Heath reached over and wrapped his arm around her shoulders. She leaned in and rested her head against his chest. She moved her button nose upward near the nape of his neck and inhaled the salty scent of musk and dirt. Kathy ran her hand down his chest, along the nylon braces that attached to his wool trousers. She listened to the soft beating of his heart against his linen shirt. As Kathy was dozing off against his chest she heard soft footsteps approach. She looked up to find Mary carrying Kira on the side of her hip.

"There you are child, you best be getting ready and the like. We need all the help we can get for the Midnight Circus after supper."

Kathy nodded and looked up at Heath. "I'll see you soon then."

He stroked her head. "Ay, see you soon."

Kathy stood up and followed Kira and Mary out of the woods and toward her caravan.

"If you're quick you might be able to catch up with the girls before their bath." Kathy watched the three girls climb down the caravan's steps carrying towels in their hands. Birgitta looked over, her blue silk scarf tied around her neck. She rolled her eyes and walked away. Moira held back and called, "Hurry up, if you want to come with us."

Kathy waved goodbye to Mary and Kira and followed the girls through the woods and down to the river. They walked along its bank for at least fifteen minutes before stopping and dropping their towels on a rocky shore. Kathy listened to their chatter and gossip. Birgitta was offering some sharp criticism to Fallon about wearing her hair so straight, saying how it made her face look long with dread.

The three of them approached the edge of the water and started to take off their clothes. Kathy slowly removed her shoes and stockings, watching as they continued their gossiping even as they became completely naked in front of each other. Kathy had dressed and bathed in front of other girls before at the orphanage but it was always in the dark or in the morning, when the others knew to avert their eyes and pretend otherwise. But here Birgitta was talking to Moira while her full breasts were completely bare, gently swaying as she moved forward to point to a beauty mark on Moira's bare stomach and comment that she was a witch. They were unashamed of their bodies as they all walked into the cold river and, with a bar of soap, they scrubbed their skin until it was a rough red.

"Are you coming?" called Moira, before she dunked the back of her head into the river. Kathy looked around nervously. She was afraid someone would be watching from between the trees. She looked down at her clothes and knew she desperately needed a wash. Kathy took a deep breath and unwrapped her skirt, unveiling her cotton, lavender pants. She unbuttoned her white blouse and removed her bra, revealing her small firm breasts. She pushed her hair forward to cover her nipples that were piercing the cold air. Quickly, she pulled her pants off to reveal the light brown hair between her legs before rushing into the river. She cringed at the coldness against her skin but the shame of the hair between her legs gave her strength to push through and move to the centre where the water came up to her waist. Her teeth chattered as she approached the group.

"Haven't you ever bathed in a river before?"

Birgitta asked, washing the last suds from her hair. Kathy shook her head.

"I guess you're one of those Travellers that just uses a cloth and bowl. This is better for your skin," she explained, matter-of-factly.

"And Birgitta likes to make her skin extra soft for Braden," Moira teased, stroking Birgitta's arm.

"Feck off," Birgitta called, splashing water in her direction.

"Here, you'll need this," Fallon said to Kathy,

passing her a bar of soap. Kathy whispered thanks under her breath and started to rub the bar against her body. She moved the hard soap through her long, tangled hair. She felt the sweet relief as the fat from the bar broke up the oil on her scalp that had built up over the weeks. She moved it to her face and arms and submerged it into the river and moved it against the other parts hidden in its dark waters. After Kathy washed her body, she watched the soap suds make their way down the river, leaving a cool stream of new water to cleanse their bodies.

There was something freeing about washing in the middle of the river, completely bare to the world around her. Kathy looked at the line of trees on either side that kept them hidden from the world. She watched as the three girls pulled back each other's hair and started to plait. Kathy looked at Birgitta's body and felt a pang of jealousy. Her silhouette was a perfect hourglass shape. Her hips were wide and rounded that led to a perfectly firm bottom. Her breasts were full and bare as Moira pulled back her hair. She was completely unaware of this and continued to plait Fallon's hair.

Kathy felt embarrassed and pushed her hair firmly over her own small breasts. She looked down at her boyish body, at her hips that were too narrow, at her waist that wasn't small enough. She ran her hands down her flat stomach and moved them to her bony hips. She lifted her head up and felt the cool wind caress her face. She wondered what it would feel like if Heath were touching her now.

"Are you going to spend the rest of the day just

staring up at those clouds?" Birgitta called, before whispering something to Fallon that made them both giggle. Kathy followed them to the riverbed. When she reached the bank, her teeth were chattering; the sun had retreated behind some clouds.

"Here," Moira said as she passed Kathy a towel.

"Thanks," Kathy replied, relieved to wrap the fabric around her bare body.

"You might want to wash those clothes now with the soap. You had a wool dress too, didn't you? I brought it here." Kathy looked down at the folded dress that sat on top of the pile of clothes.

"I also noticed your stockings had holes in them so I thought you could use these," she offered, handing her a pair of long wool socks.

"Th... thank you," Kathy replied, touched by Moira's kindness. The other girls in their wrapped towels picked up their clothes and walked into the shallow part of the river. While squatting, they submerged their garments into the water, rubbing the soap vigorously into the fabric. Kathy picked up her own items and mirrored their actions. When they finished, they all dressed into their set of dry, clean clothes.

Afterwards, Birgitta, Fallon and Moira packed their wet clothing items with precision, rolled into their towels, to help them dry until they could be hung near the stove in their caravan. Birgitta delicately tied her blue silk scarf around her head to cover her wet hair. Moira collected the bars of soap into a tin bucket. Together, the four of them walked back to their caravan through the forest; their bodies clean and bonded by the shared waters in the river.

When they arrived at the caravan, they unpacked their wet clothes and hung it on the rope that lined the interior of the room. After hanging their items, Moira, Fallon and Birgitta left to have supper before the first guests arrived. Kathy finished hanging her pants next to the stove when she caught her reflection in the mirror. She looked at her bare knees and thighs. Her torn stockings were left behind at the river and replaced with the wool socks Moira gave her. She frowned at the sight of her bare knees and thighs and attempted to pull the wool socks up even higher. But no matter how far she pulled them, she still felt naked.

While Kathy was staring at herself in the mirror, she heard a soft knock coming from the door. Kathy opened the top half of it and found Heath standing on the other side. He looked freshly bathed. His dark, curly hair, still wet, glistened in the evening sun. His tweed waistcoat was worn over a bright white shirt, his trousers were neatly buckled, and he wore a shiny pair of Oxfords on his feet.

He lifted his arms. "What do you think?" he asked with a crooked smile, as he turned around.

Kathy smiled. "You look great."

Heath eyed her dress. His eyes followed her silhouette down her torso to her legs and then up again. She felt her cheeks blush.

"You look beautiful in that dress," he said, holding out his hand for her to join him on the platform outside the door. She took it and closed the door on the warm room behind her.

"Don't be daft, my knees look gnarly in this dress," she said, attempting to pull the dress lower and socks higher. Neither worked so she settled on crossing her arms around her body instead.

They walked to the centre of the camp and took a seat next to each other near the fire. Heath moved his hand and placed it on her thigh, he moved it down over her knee. "What's so gnarly about these knees?" he asked.

Kathy felt her stomach tighten, the skin where his hand touched her was burning with a tingling sensation. She brushed his hand away. "Watch where you put that," she said, eyeing him playfully.

He kissed the top of her head before standing up. He walked over to Bree, who clumsily offered him two bowls of stew. When he arrived back at the fire he offered Kathy one which she accepted gratefully.

"Are you nervous?" Kathy asked, taking a spoonful of beef and vegetables.

Heath shrugged. "I've done it enough times before." He tucked into the stew in front of him. They ate silently while the other Travellers around them transformed the camp. They packed away all personal and sentimental items, piling things into their caravans or wagons. Bree made a poor attempt at hanging streamers between the vehicles. Laoise's caravan had white candles all around it, leading up to the small table covered in black cloth where her tarot cards waited to be read.

"The camp really changes for the Midnight Circus,

doesn't it?" Kathy asked, amazed at how differently things now looked.

"A lot of people are afraid of settlers, you see. They don't want them knowing what goes on inside our camps or caravans. They try to keep it staged as much as they can. Just showing them what they need to see." Kathy thought about the nuns at the orphanage and how they kept outsiders away. And in the rare occasions when they'd have a Bishop visit, the girls were given new uniforms and expected to behave.

Heath leaned in closer and whispered, "The camp packs up after the Midnight Circus and rides through the night. We should reach Athlone in the morning. Once we're there and everyone's busy unpacking, we can slip away. I've already arranged it with Kieran."

Kathy nodded. "I'll be ready."

"I'm going to pack while everyone's out of here, I'll see you in an hour." He squeezed her hand tightly before standing up and walking to his tent. Kathy looked up from her half eaten stew. Everyone around her looked their best, with most of the dirt washed away to reveal their sun-aged skin.

Courtney walked up next to Kathy and laid out a variety of bread onto the table. Looking satisfied with herself, she flattened her apron and went back to the large pot of stew that sat on the fire's coals and gave it a stir. Kathy had only stayed with the Travellers for four weeks but she was beginning to get used to their rituals. How they served their coffees in the morning with a conscious thought, and the small groups that would form around the great fire at meal times.

Everyone had their place. As Kathy looked at all the groups around her, chatting excitedly about tonight's activities Kathy tried to picture where Heath would normally sit. Would he be with Tommy and Kieran? Leaning against a wagon and pointing to the different horses as they spoke. Kathy looked over quickly to Birgitta's group, with Braden and Moira on either side of her, and Fallon on the end. She couldn't picture him sitting next to them. Perhaps he would eat with Sloane and Cian, who were sharing their meal next to some older Travellers. Kathy felt a pang in her heart when she thought of Heath leaving these groups. What would tomorrow morning look like without him? She swallowed and stood up, leaving her unfinished stew to one side, and walked back to the caravan to pack her rucksack.

***

When Kathy arrived at the caravan, she quickly climbed up the three steps to the platform and walked into the warm room. The sight of her clothes hanging on the laundry line with the other girls' items made her smile. She reached out and touched the rough fabric between her fingers. Satisfied that both her skirt and shirt were dried, she folded them into her arms. Kathy walked over to her bed and pulled out the rucksack from underneath it. She gently placed her folded clothes and extra knickers inside of it after removing Sinead's red jumper. Kathy lifted the jumper over her head and let it fall around her body. She hugged the fabric close to her. She turned to her small pillow and lifted it, revealing an old paperback book and the leather-bound Book of Moons. She carefully placed the books at the very top of her rucksack. She closed the bag and returned it under her bed. Looking up, she noticed the small wooden box of leaves belonging to Kira and felt a pang of guilt in her stomach. She didn't want to leave Kira behind. Aside from Mary, Kathy was the only one who ever spent time with her. Kathy looked down at the threaded bracelet wrapped around her wrist and smiled.

Reaching across the bed, she picked up the box and opened the lid. Kathy lifted a small oak leaf that was beginning to brown at the edges. It reminded Kathy of a pressed book of leaves she made when she was younger. Her and Sinead would collect leaves on their way back from school to the orphanage. They'd stick them between the waxy thin pages of an old bible they stole from church, and hid it under Sinead's bed. One night before supper, they carelessly left the bible on Kathy's bed. Kathy was pulled straight from her plate and dragged by the hair into the matron's office. Kathy cringed as she remembered the force of the nun's hands shoving her skirt above her waist and throwing her to the ground. She touched the skin on the top of her thighs and bum and remembered the sting of leather against her flesh. It left welts for weeks. Kathy cried every night while Sinead held her in her arms.

"Are you ready, Kath?" Heath called from the other side of the door, pulling it open. Kathy dropped the box on the bed and quickly wiped the tears from her eyes.

"I'm ready."

"Everything okay? You look like you've been crying." Heath approached and put his arm around her shoulders.

Kathy shook her head. "I'm fine, really, it's nothing."

Heath looked at her intently. "If you're ready, Mary and Kira could use your help, our first visitors have turned up."

Kathy dried her cheeks before she whispered, "I'm ready."

***

"Are you nervous love?" Mary asked, while tying a red ribbon in Kira's long, dark hair. Kathy nodded as she laid out the jewellery pieces on a folded table they had set up earlier.

"That's normal, it's hard to interact with the settlers at first and the like but you'll get the hang of it." She lifted her hands from Kira's head and smiled.

"The most important thing is to enjoy yourself. You'll never learn a thing unless you enjoy yourself."

Kathy nodded and looked down at the bracelet tied around her wrist. She felt a wave of sadness again at the thought of leaving Kira.

"Why don't you carry this here tray of bracelets. The crowd tends to hang by the fire where they do the performances and the like." Mary pressed a wooden tray filled with bracelets into Kathy's palms.

"How much are they?" Kathy asked, noticing they didn't have prices listed next to them. Mary looked up startled from the bracelet she was beading.

"We don't have prices, we just negotiate with settlers on that sort of thing."

Kathy's cheeks burned with embarrassment. "Right, yes, I knew that." She walked away quickly from Mary and Kira.

As Kathy strolled through the crowd, she started to notice how different settled people were to the Travellers. The settlers walked around in groups and pairs, never leaving one another's side. Their clothing appeared clean and pressed, their hair neatly plaited or curled. When Kathy approached them with the tray full of jewellery she struggled to speak with any of them. She went up to a group of young girls and they just stared at her with amusement and ran off giggling with each other. While Kathy was pushing through the crowd that was lining up for the next round of coffees, she swore she saw a woman stick out her foot which made Kathy tumble to the ground and drop the tray of bracelets. Kathy cursed as she rummaged her hands through the dirt, trying to find the jewellery.

"Here, let me help," came a voice next to her. They were holding a candle. Kathy glanced up and was surprised to see Birgitta's face reflected in the flickering light.

"Thanks," Kathy mumbled. Birgitta moved the candle closer to the ground and together they picked up the pieces and placed them back onto the tray.

"It's hard the first time," she said, taking Kathy's hand and helping her up. "To be around gorgers."

Kathy looked around her and nodded.

"I'm guessing you didn't really interact with any of them in your old camp, did you?"

Kathy shook her head, feeling a twinge of guilt for lying to Birgitta.

"Do you want to sit next to me while I read some tarot? You can clean the dirt from those bracelets."

Kathy followed Birgitta to the outside of the inner circle where a long queue waited for her outside a caravan. She walked past a few impatient patrons, one in particular mumbled, 'bout time gypo,' to which Birgitta whispered in response, "I look forward to telling him when he's going to die."

While Kathy brushed the dirt from the pieces of jewellery, she watched Birgitta read the fortunes of strangers in the setting sunlight. The candlelight danced around her table as her small fingers caressed each card she turned over. Kathy watched the soft silk, that was wrapped around her neck, move gently in the evening wind. Her freshly washed blonde hair waved slightly down to her waist. On more than one occasion, she was approached by groups of young men, eager to have their cards read to tell them whether she'd go on a date with any of them. She brushed them off, ignoring their comments, and shooed them away before beckoning the next customer.

"I'd better be off, I need to sell these for Mary." Birgitta ignored her as she held a card close to her face.

The camp was dark now, except for the bright full moon that peaked from the clouds to illuminate its surroundings in silver light. Kathy avoided the groups of young girls and instead found her luck with couples, who were often eager to buy their date a token of affection. When Kathy returned to Mary with her empty tray, she found her humming quietly to herself, with only a few pieces remaining on the table. Kira was curled up in a small ball, sleeping soundly on a blanket on the ground.

"That's grand love," Mary replied, taking the tray from Kathy. "I can finish the rest here if you'd like to see some performances and the like." Kathy smiled and walked back to the centre fire where, off to the side, they had constructed a small stage made from tree stumps and branches tied together with rope. Heath had just started to play. His body moved with the music. It was magical seeing him play in the moonlight. His head lifted to the stars, his mouth in a soft, crooked smile. A smile that knew he held the world in every beat. He kept his eyes closed and his feet kept him in rhythm, his body swaying with every note. The audience was captivated and when it ended they applauded and whistled. While they clapped, Paddy went around the crowd with his upturned flat cap in hand and waited for people to drop their coins into it. He gave Kathy a quick wink as he walked past. Kathy smiled and admired Heath, who had started another song. She looked to the side and noticed Sloane in a small green velvet dress, stretching her limbs for her dance number. Kathy moved on, she didn't want Sloane to catch her watching in the audience.

***

Kathy walked back to Birgitta, but when she reached the table it was empty and no one was standing in the queue to have their cards read. Kathy figured most people had moved to the centre of the camp to watch the performances. She smiled to herself as she listened to the music Heath was making. She had just closed her eyes and was swaying to the sound when she heard shouting from behind a caravan. The voice sounded like Birgitta's. Kathy listened closely to what she thought were male voices too. Kathy's heart started to speed up. She crept behind the caravan and saw three young men surrounding Birgitta. They were pushing her between them as she shouted at them to stop. When she raised her arms to push them back the two taller men grabbed her wrists and pulled them tightly behind her.

"Don't touch me," she hissed, spitting on the ground at the heavier man's feet. He backed away laughing, as he stumbled slightly in his drunkenness.

"I heard pikeys were rough, but I wonder what they look like underneath all those clothes." The other two chuckled in agreement, pulling her arms tighter against her sides as she squirmed harder to escape their grasp. He walked closer and stroked her wavy hair with his rough hand, she turned her head and bit down on it with such a force he screamed and moved away.

"Bitch!" he shouted, slapping her across the face. Kathy dropped to the ground and moved her hands on the dirt searching for something hard. The second man let go of Birgitta's wrist and pulled her to the ground by the scarf around her throat. She gasped for air, chocking against its pull. As she moved her hands to the scarf around her neck, the heavier man ripped the front of her dress. Her pale breasts lay bare in the moonlight as the men started to unbuckle their belts. Birgitta's hands fumbled around the scarf until she was able to untie the bow. She gasped for air as the two men pinned her wrists against the earth.

Kathy's hands finally found a large rock. She stood up quickly and while the heavier man was now attempting to pull Birgitta's pants down her squirming body Kathy ran behind him and hit the large rock against his skull. He shouted in excruciating pain, taking both hands to his head to steady himself. The other two looked up, and as if awoken from some kind of spell, they released Birgitta and stumbled against one another on the ground trying to get up. Kathy grabbed Birgitta's hand and pulled her away from the men. The heavier man shouted and stumbled his way to his feet, following the other two quickly through the woods and away from the camp. Birgitta had her arms around her breasts and her hair covered in dirt and twigs.

"Thank you," she whispered, her teeth chattering as her entire body shivered. Kathy pulled her red jumper off and lifted it above Birgitta's head, who raised her arms and slipped into its warmth. Kathy wrapped her arms around Birgitta as she cried in Kathy's shoulder. "I'm so sorry Birgitta. I wish I got here sooner. I tried to stop it as soon as I could."

"No," Birgitta shook her head. She pulled away

from Kathy. "Don't feel sorry for me."

"I didn't mean it like that, it's just, you don't deserve this. You must feel awful and I'm sorry."

"You don't know what it feels like," she spat, her arms hugging the red wool against her body tightly.

"You have no idea what this feels like!" she shouted. Kathy closed her eyes. She remembered that night when Sinead ran into the dormitory. She threw herself into Kathy's bed crying. Kathy held her as Sinead recounted what happened when she stayed late in the chapel, helping the priest set up for Easter service the next morning. The smell of incense and damp in his office. The weight of his heavy body. Kathy felt helpless as she held her friend, knowing there was nothing she could do to make it better. Their only choice was to run. Find a way to escape to Dublin together and make a new life. Kathy looked down at the blue silk scarf that was marked with the man's boot. She wiped warm tears from her eyes.

"You're right, I don't know what it feels like," she whispered.

"Birgitta, are you okay?" Moira shouted, rushing over with Fallon behind her.

"What happened? You look terrible." Fallon removed a twig from her hair.

"It's nothing."

"Did she do this?" Fallon asked, looking down at Kathy, who was still sitting in the dirt. Birgitta shook her head.

"Let's just go," Moira said. She wrapped her arms around Birgitta while Fallon continued to pick the dirt and twigs from her hair. They walked away, leaving Kathy on the ground. Kathy closed her eyes tightly and felt the moonlight against her eyelids.

"Kath, are you okay?" someone whispered, gently shaking her shoulder. Kathy opened her eyes and saw Heath kneeling next to her. She looked down at her hands and noticed she was still clutching Birgitta's blue scarf.

"I... I'm fine," she stuttered, looking up at Heath. "I need to wash this," Kathy said, standing up slowly and looking around her. Most of the caravans were now packed away. There were just a few kitchen items left to be stowed in the wagon next to them. "I need to wash this," Kathy explained, moving towards the woods.

"Kath, wait up!" Heath called, jogging to catch up to her long strides. "Where are you going?"

Kathy ignored his calls and followed the moonlit path to the river bed. When she arrived at the river, she walked into the shallow part of the water. She felt the cold rush over her shoes and up to her ankles. She knelt on the rocks and plunged the silk scarf into the water. With both hands, she vigorously rubbed the scarf against itself.

"Kath, it's freezing in there." Heath reached for her shoulder to pull her back but she shrugged him off and continued to plunge the scarf into the water as she whispered, "I need to make it clean again."

Desperate to get Kathy's attention, Heath trudged into the river and knelt in front of her. He grabbed her wrists and met her eyes.

"What happened, Kathy?" he asked slowly, surveying her pale face.

"I need to make it clean again," she pleaded. An uncontrollable sob escaped her lips and she felt her body crumble against his, as she cried into his shoulders. She clutched the scarf to her chest and he rocked her in the riverbed. She looked down at her naked wrist and realised the bracelet Kira had made for her had fallen into the river. She pushed Heath back and dipped her hands into the water again. She moved the rocks on the bottom of the river, trying to find the tiny beads of red and purple below the surface.

"Kath, we have to go," Heath explained softly.

He moved his arms underneath her and lifted her small body against his. Submissively, Kathy gave in to his warm body and wrapped her wet arms around his neck. Heath carried her away from the river and through the woods. When they arrived back at the camp, only the wagon was left behind. It was strange to see the clearing empty, with only the imprints of caravan wheels, leaving behind their ghostly presence. Heath lifted Kathy gently into the wagon before climbing up himself. Kathy studied the things around her. The wagon reminded her of the one she fell asleep in just a month earlier. Heath pulled the rough canvas over their bodies, revealing the same clattering pots. He gave a quick nod to the man in the front of the wagon that looked like Paddy. He tipped his cap and placed his pipe in his mouth. While grabbing the reins of the horse, he pulled them forward with a jolt. Heath removed his wool blazer and wrapped it around

Kathy's shoulders. Kathy opened her clenched fist and gazed down at the sodden silk scarf. She lifted it to the moonlight. The stains were now gone and in the morning, when it was dried, it would be like nothing ever happened.

"Sing me a song Heath," Kathy asked, as she laid her head against his chest and listened to his heartbeat. Heath leaned his head against the top of her forehead and, in his soft voice, he sang the night away.

Chapter Seven

The Fort

Kathy was back at the orphanage. Sitting on her small bed, she had Sinead's head on her lap and was stroking her red curls.

"We'll meet at St. Stephens Green," Sinead said, before turning on her stomach and looking up at Kathy. "It's where my ma' used to take me when I was young. There's a lovely stone bridge that crosses over a pond."

Kathy frowned. "We won't get separated. I wish you'd stop talking about this."

Sinead knelt up and grabbed both of Kathy's hands. "I know that Kath but if anything happens, I want you to keep going." Sinead's eyes filled with tears, she turned to look at the row of beds next to hers.

Kathy hugged her tightly. "We'll get out, don't worry. I'll find us a way out." Kathy wiped the teardrops from her face.

"What time?"

Sinead glanced up. "Time?"

"What time will we meet on the bridge?"

She smiled and replied, "Eleven, we'll meet at the bridge at eleven in the morning."

Kathy smiled and looked away, a flash of dark hair appeared near the door.

"Kira? What are you doing here?" Kathy asked,

standing up from the bed and walking to the door where Kira walked through a few seconds earlier. Kathy expected to find Kira on the landing outside the dormitory. But Kathy didn't enter the corridor. Instead she was by the river, watching Kira on the moonlit bank searching through some stones.

"I lost something. Can you help me find it?" Kira asked.

Kathy walked over and knelt next to Kira. She picked up the stones one at a time before tossing them aside.

"What am I looking for?" Kathy asked.

"It's a story stone."

Kathy looked down again and picked up a large flat stone. It shone brightly in the moonlight. There were markings across the surface. It looked like a bird.

"Is this it?" Kathy asked, showing the bright stone to Kira. She beamed and picked it up before quickly placing it in her pocket.

"It's time Kath, it's time to wake up."

Kathy's eyes darted open. She squinted in the darkness, trying to see her surroundings. She could make out the shape of someone next to her.

"What's happening?" Kathy mumbled, rubbing her eyes and finding Heath next to her. He put his finger to his lips and nodded at Paddy and Cian whispering to one another.

"One of the wheels on a caravan broke, we're moving to the nearest field," Heath whispered, nudging himself closer to Kathy.

"Why do you look so nervous? It's just another

field."

Heath shook his head. "It's not, I think we're in Templemaley..." Heath looked up at Paddy, who waved to Cian before beckoning the horse forward.

"We're in front of the Ballycarroll Caher, a fairy fort, an infamous one. All the Travellers know to stay clear away from here." They felt the jolt of the wagon climb a kerb and up into the field where it stopped a few metres forward. When they parked, Heath sat up and climbed down from the wagon. He held out his hand to help Kathy and then walked over to Paddy.

"Here Heath, take Rua to Kieran. I need to help the lads with the caravans." Heath nodded and grabbed the horse's reins from Paddy.

"He's spooked," Heath said, as he reached for the horse's forehead before patting it gently. Rua trotted the ground nervously. They walked with her into the open field and found Kieran in the distance pulling three horses. Kathy surveyed her new surroundings.

The landscape was wide and open. A morning fog rested on the grass. Kathy felt the dew against her ankles. To the far left, she saw a river run behind a ring of trees.

"Is that the fort?" Kathy asked, looking at the trees in the distance.

Heath nodded and waved to Kieran who approached them.

"Ah thank God you're here Heath, I've been having an awful time trying to calm down these beasts."

Heath nodded. "Ay, they know better than to be here."

Kieran handed some saddle reins to Heath and Kathy. "Can you take them down to the river? I need to get the others." Heath peered nervously toward the fort.

"Take the path ahead of you and continue straight, it'll bring you to the river. Whatever you do, don't take the right path, it looks shorter but it'll bring you to the fort." He waved again and jogged over to the group of caravans that were arranging themselves into a tight circle that would keep them protected through the night.

Kathy and Heath walked the horses down to the river. When they reached the edge, Kathy released the reins so the horses could drink from the cool stream of water. The tabby horse gently nudge the white one aside to dip its mouth into the river first. Kathy and Heath sat on a rock by the riverbed and waited for Kieran to join them and exchange a few of their thirsty horses for the ones that had their share. By the time all the horses had been watered and let out into the field to graze, the mist had begun to evaporate. The sky was brighter, the birds were louder, and the smell of fire and coffee beans roasting filled the air.

They walked their tired legs up to the centre of the field and squeezed themselves through a small gap between the caravans to the large fire where Bree was pouring the contents of her tin kettle into mugs. She handed them awkwardly to Courtney who in return snatched them impatiently. Kathy and Heath stood back as they watched the morning ritual unfold. Laoise approached them, wearing her long, black dress with beaded necklaces weighing down her small neck. She walked up to Courtney, who handed her the steaming cup, and Laoise inhaled the aromas before taking a long sip. Next to Courtney were two men Kathy had never seen before. The first appeared very old, his hair thin and grey. He leaned against a walking stick while he held a pipe in his other hand. The second appeared to be the same age as Paddy, but his auburn hair had begun to thin. It was combed back with a gloss that made it shine in the morning light. His skin was like leather, from the years he had spent in the sun, and his nose was slightly crooked.

He moved his hand into a small pouch and poured some coins into Laoise's palm. She gave him a short nod and walked a few feet in front of the fire where her old caravan and cat waited for her. She kept the door open just a while longer to let the black feline in before closing it gently behind her. Kathy watched this repeat, where people approached to receive their morning coffee and then a handful of coins from the thuggish man next to Courtney.

"Who are they?" Kathy asked, as Braden walked up to the auburn haired man. He gave the old man a soft punch on the arm before accepting his money.

Heath rolled his eyes before leaning in closer to Kathy to whisper. "That one handing out coins is Johnny Connors, they call him the King of the Travellers. He was a famous boxer in his day before he retired years ago." Heath nodded looking up at him. "I'm not sure about the other one, don't think he's come around here before.

"I've never seen them before in the camp."

"You wouldn't have; Johnny's really a tinker now. Spends most of his time on the road. Going through towns selling off the tin kettles and cups Leary and Niall make. He's the one that always finds us a good deal for our horses. Sometimes he's away for weeks but yer man keeps him in line," Heath said, nodding his head toward Courtney. "He gets our meat and food from the towns around our camp, so he's never gone very long."

"Why is he giving money to everyone?"

"That's from last night. He goes around collecting what people made from the Midnight Circus and gives them a portion back. It's how we pay for our supplies."

Kathy watched Mary walk up and receive her mug of coffee. She didn't stop to look at Johnny and walked away without any coins.

"But Mary, she sold loads of jewellery last night, why isn't she getting anything?"

Heath stared awkwardly down at his feet, shuffling them against the dirt. "Some people have to pay more to stay here," he answered, not making eye contact with her.

"But that doesn't seem fair, Mary worked really hard making that jewellery and for that matter so did I," Kathy snapped, folding her arms across her chest. Heath reached out to touch her but she backed away.

"So how much do you make then?"

Heath ran his hand through his dark hair and rolled his eyes. "It doesn't matter Kath, I'm not nearly as important as others in the clan."

"Important? So I guess I'm not important at all, huh? Or Mary?"

"That's not what I'm saying Kath, it's just the way things are here. Siders don't make any money, okay?" Heath threw his arms in the air and walked off angrily, leaving Kathy behind in her own rage. She felt anger bubble in her belly. She took in a rattled breath, trying to keep it back. Kathy dug her hands deep into her dress pockets and felt the soft caress of the silk scarf. She looked over to Mary, who was watching Kira play with some stones on the ground next to the fire. Kathy didn't understand it. What made Laoise better than Mary? They both contributed to the

Midnight Circus and helped out in their own way.

Mary looked up and saw Kathy watching, she gestured for her to join them. Kathy took another breath in and felt her rage slowly dissipate.

"Mornin' love, did you enjoy last night and the like?"

Kathy took a seat next to Mary. "It was fine," Kathy replied, pushing the thought of Birgitta from her mind.

The two women watched Kira stack stones on top of one another until they tumbled down again. Kathy crawled closer to her and placed a small stone on top of the pile.

"I had a dream about you last night Kira," Kathy said, looking down at the stone in her hand. "You were picking up stones just like these but we were near the river and it was night time." Kathy looked at the stone pile before turning to face Kira. Kira was fumbling with the last stone in her palm. She looked up to Kathy and smiled before passing her the flat rock. Kathy accepted it and looked down at the smooth surface on her palm. Kathy's stomach turned when she saw the same etching of a bird she had seen in her dream.

"Did you dream it too?" Kathy whispered in disbelief. Kira smiled before picking herself up and walking over to Mary. Mary hummed gently as she stroked Kira's dark hair. Kathy shook her head and stood up from the ground. She brushed the dirt from her knees while she quickly mumbled, "I need to go." Kathy felt her heart against her chest. What could it mean? She wondered, feeling the stone clasped tightly in her palm. She needed to find Heath to tell him about it.

Kathy walked through the camp and saw a few of the men pull together a bender tent. She walked over as Braden dug some branches into the earth.

"Mornin'," Braden called, standing straight and wiping the dirt on his white under-shirt. "Looking for your boyfriend?" he asked, throwing her a look before tying the canvas to the branch.

"He's not my boyfriend," Kathy mumbled, crossing her arms.

"Whatever he is, he's not here helping us build this bender. He's down by the river."

"Thanks." Kathy started to walk away before turning around again. "Is Birgitta okay, Braden?" she asked. His body froze. He stood up and glanced over his shoulder.

"She's fine. We just need to forget the whole thing.

Leave it Kathy." He walked around the shelter to attach the canvas to some other branches.

Kathy dropped the stone into her dress pocket and walked to the part of the river where, that morning, Heath and Kathy had watered the horses. She lifted her face and felt the August sun wash over her. When she followed the path to the riverbed, she found Heath skipping stones. Kathy stood behind a tree. The sun hit his dark curls and his arm muscles flexed when he threw the stones into the river. There was a boyish look to him, with his sleeves rolled up to his elbows, his feet bare and his trousers turned up to his calves. He appeared peaceful in the midsummer afternoon. She saw the small trickles of sweat drop down from his hairline and onto his back. Kathy felt the heat of the sun beat down on her wool dress. She felt it stick against her skin. She bent forward to take her shoes off and pulled the wool stockings down her calves and off her feet. The relief of her bare skin on the grass felt refreshing. She picked up her shoes and walked down to Heath.

"I'm busy," he mumbled to the footsteps behind him, as he threw a rock in the river. Kathy set her shoes down and walked behind him. She pulled his arm back as he reached up to throw another stone. His skin felt hot like hers. She moved in front of him and ran her fingers through his curly, dark hair. She stood up on her tiptoes so her lips could reach his. He pressed back eagerly. She ran her hands down his back which was wet with sweat. She pulled his body close to hers, their mouths moving rhythmically, their tongues tasting the saltiness of each other.

Kathy's hands met the front of his open shirt and she pulled it off his shoulders. She felt the contours of each muscle as the linen moved down his arms. He found the hem of her wool dress and pulled it over her body, revealing her bare breasts and cotton pants. She pulled away to smile shyly before reaching for his trouser button and the zip that released them from his hips. He stepped from his trousers and together in a bare embrace they felt the sun beat against their backs. Kathy pulled away and took his hand. She led him to the river and tentatively they walked into its waters. The cold water was a shock and then a relief from the hot sun. With Heath in hand, she walked deeper into the water, stopping where it rested at her waist. She felt the cool surrender through her body and turned to face him.

He moved his hands through her auburn hair and followed the waves to her shoulders. He ran his fingers down her chest and cupped her small breasts with his callused hands. She tilted her head as she felt his fingers run over her nipples that hardened at his touch. His hands moved down her stomach to her navel, to her hips and lower back where he pulled her in closer and their lips met again. She moved her hands over the hairs of his chest, down to the top of his boxers. She felt her heart beat against her chest, her breath quickening, his body eager to meet hers.

When they pulled away she laid her head against his shoulder.

***

"I wish we could lay here forever," Heath sighed, pulling Kathy closer to his body. Kathy outlined the contours of Heath's chest as she laid in his arms. They had spent the last hour in the grass, their bodies drying in the mid-afternoon sun. Heath nuzzled his nose into her hair.

"Me too."

"How long will it take to fix the caravan's wheel?"

Heath chuckled and pulled her body closer to his. "Are you eager to leave?"

Kathy felt her cheeks blush. "I'm worried about Sinead. What if she's already in Dublin waiting for me?"

"She'll wait for you."

Kathy sat up and folded her knees to her chest. "We always talked about what we would do if we got separated. I just never really expected it to happen." She burrowed her forehead between her knees and took a deep breath in. "We said we'd meet at St. Stephens Green, on the stone bridge that crosses the pond. That we'd go there every morning at eleven until we saw each other."

Heath reached out and pushed her hair behind her ear. "You'll find her again, Kath. I know you will." He kissed the top of her head before standing up and pulling his trousers on.

"In a few days we'll have the wheel fixed and we'll be on our way to Athlone. Once we're there, we'll be straight on our way to Dublin. It's much faster when you're not stopping every ten miles to setup camp."

Kathy nodded, and pulled her wool dress over her body. It felt rough against her skin compared to the soft grass they had laid on just a few moments earlier. Kathy felt something heavy against her leg and slipped her hand inside her pocket. She felt the smooth surface of the stone. She pulled it out and held it up against the sun. The white markings sparkled in the midsummer light.

"What's that?" Heath asked, looking over.

Kathy told him about the dream she had. How she found Kira stacking stones that morning by the fire that it was the same stone she had dreamt about.

"Do you know what it means?" Kathy asked.

Heath let out a long sigh. "Could be an omen of some sort."

"Do you think it's something bad?"

Heath picked up the stone and looked at it. "It doesn't feel bad."

Kathy nodded and placed the stone back into her pocket.

"I wouldn't worry about it too much, it's probably just a coincidence." Heath grabbed her hand and together they walked through the small woods and stepped out into the open field. Kathy held her shoes in her hand and felt the grass stroke her ankles.

"There ye are Heath," came a voice from behind. Kathy and Heath turned to find the two men Kathy saw earlier that morning handing out coins. Johnny now had a flat cap covering his hair; he held onto the reins of his tabby horse. The second man was smoking a pipe while leaning against his wagon. Johnny nodded to Heath before he reached into his deep pockets and pulled out a handful of coins. Heath reached out and accepted the money before hastily putting the coins into his own pocket.

"You off again then, Johnny?" Heath asked, looking up at the wagon ahead and the horse that had a packed bag attached to its saddle.

"Ay, going up to Belfast. You shan't be seeing me again, I plan to settle there and support the Provos for as long as they need." Heath nodded. Johnny's eyes met Kathy's again.

"This is Kathy, she's new to the camp."

"Ay." He held out his hand which Kathy shook. "Yer eyes, they look familiar is all, they remind me of a Traveller girl I knew long ago."

Kathy looked away, feeling uncomfortable with the attention.

Heath cleared his throat and shook Johnny's hand again. "Tabhair aire," he said.

Johnny nodded and pulled himself up on his horse and tipped his cap. "Dhalyōn mun'ia," he replied, before beckoning the horse forward into a trot.

"What was that?" Kathy asked, unfamiliar with his response.

"Shelta, it's the language of Travellers."

Heath watched the man on the horse disappear down the country lane. He pulled Kathy into his arms and whispered, "Gra a mo gris."

Kathy giggled and turned to face him. "That better be something nice."

"It means love of my heart."

***

The following afternoon Kathy sat by the fire, reading her old book. Mary approached her with Kira on her heels, tugging at her skirt with pleading eyes.

"Oh Kathy, would you mind bringing Kira down to the woods? She wants to collect some leaves but I told Courtney I would go into town with her."

"Sure," Kathy said, as she closed her book and placed it on the bench. She held out her hand as she walked up to Kira. Eagerly, the little girl took it. Kathy bent down and pushed back a dark strand of hair from Kira's smiling face.

"Shall we collect some leaves?"

Kira smiled back and nodded eagerly.

"Take care not to go near that fort," Mary called after them.

Kathy waved goodbye to Mary and followed Kira's pull toward the river. She followed her through the caravans and into the field. Kira's tugs were persistent and strong. Kathy's arm started to ache but she followed the girl's determined steps across the clearing and through the trees. Kira followed the river from the path and stopped in front of a bunch of trees near the water. Kathy released Kira's hand. She ran up to the trees and started to collect their fallen leaves. Kathy sat on the grassy bank and watched Kira's small hands hold up a Hawthorne leaf. Satisfied with her selection, she ran over to Kathy and dropped it onto her lap before running back to collect some more. Kira's black hair swayed in the cool breeze. The sky was getting darker from the thick, blue clouds and the wind had begun to pick up. Kira tiptoed on her bare feet to reach a leaf from a taller branch, only to fall on her backside. Kathy crunched the pile of leaves into her palm and scrambled to her feet to assist Kira. The leftover leaves from her lap were catching in the wind and rushing past them into the river.

"C'mon Kira," Kathy called, beckoning the girl to follow her. Kira stared into the water and watched her leaves float down the river.

"Kira," Kathy called again, raising her voice sternly. Kira smiled and approached Kathy. She held her hands open and Kathy placed the pile of leaves into her palms. Kira held them tightly as they followed the river back to the path that led to the field. As they walked up a small incline, Kira ran ahead of Kathy, throwing her leaves onto the ground in the process. Her small feet ran to the fork in the path that led to the fairy fort.

"Kira, don't go that way!" Kathy yelled after her. The wind had started to pick up and whipped Kathy's hair in her eyes. It had begun to rain, making the path slippery. Kathy followed Kira down the path, her small silhouette moving closer to the circle of trees ahead of her.

The trees whipped their branches frantically in the air; the wind was so strong Kathy was sure she might be picked up and thrown back at any moment.

"We need to turn back, it's raining!" Kathy called as Kira continued to run ahead of her. She sped up and finally caught up to Kira. Kathy was about to reach her hand to grab Kira's shoulder when she heard a voice she recognised from behind the trees. The voice called her name. Kathy froze. She looked between the trees where it had come from. The rain started to fall heavier, obscuring her view.

"Sinead?" Kathy called timidly into the shadows. "Is that you?"

From the corner of her eye Kathy caught a glimpse of a curly red head move behind a tree. Kathy ran into the trees.

"Sinead... wait!"

"Kath!" Kathy turned as Heath ran towards her in the rain. His hair wet against his head. "They've fixed the wheel, we're getting ready to leave; are you okay? You look pale." He grabbed her by the shoulders. Kathy was still staring at the place where she had seen the figure. She pointed to the trees.

"I swear I saw Sinead just now," Kathy whispered. She stared at the spot where the red mass of curls were just a moment ago. Kathy inspected the empty space, walking back and forth around the trees. But nothing was there except tree branches crashing into one another in the wind.

"But that's impossible, no one else is here," Heath said.

Kathy walked around the trees for the third time. "No one else... but me and Kira. Kira's here...

Heath where's Kira?" Kathy's heart raced. She walked quickly back onto the path. Her heart stopped when she couldn't see the shape of Kira in the distance.

"Kira, where are you?" Kathy shouted, running along the path.

"Kath, come back... you can't go down that way! That's where the fairy fort is!" Heath called after her. Kathy turned and moved her soaked hair from her face. "Kira must be down here," she yelled through the wind and rain.

Heath ran up to her, his face as pale as Kathy's. "Which way did she go?"

"I don't know, she was running this way and then... then I heard Sinead call for me in the trees." Kathy ran her hands through her hair frantically looking around. She felt nauseas. The trees were towering over her and she began to feel like they were closing in on them.

"We'll find her," Heath said reassuringly, wiping the rain from his face. "I'll go down to the river and you keep to the path. Whatever you do, don't go into the fort!"

Heath quickly climbed down the path and onto the riverbank. Kathy continued forward, keeping her eyes peeled for the small head of dark hair. She walked along the path for a few more minutes, calling Kira's name. Nervously, she glanced up at the ring of trees that towered ahead of her.

"Kathy, quick, down here!" She heard Heath shout, faintly. Kathy ran down from the path, onto the muddy hill that led to the river's edge. When she arrived, Kathy saw the rain pounding the water around a small body floating face down, caught in the river reeds. The small frame gently moved with the river's current, a blanket of elm and maple leaves surrounded her shape. Kathy screamed and ran into the river as Heath fought his way though the thick mud to get to Kira's body. Kathy fell to her knees when Heath pulled her out of the water. Her skin was pale and her eyes looked like they wouldn't open. Heath laid Kira's body gently onto the bank and pushed on her chest. When she didn't move, he turned her around and tried to pat the water out of her lungs. She lay lifeless in his arms. He looked up at Kathy with tears in his eyes.

"I'm so sorry, she's gone now," he sobbed.

Kathy felt her body convulse uncontrollably. She shook her head and crawled over.

"She can't be," she cried. "She's just sleeping... look how her eyes are shut. Please God, she's just sleeping," Kathy pleaded, touching Kira's cold face.

"Wake up Kira. You need to wake up," Kathy cried, gently nudging her small shoulders.

Heath shook his head. "They took her Kath," he croaked, looking up at the ring of trees only a few feet away from them. "She's gone now, she's gone home." He rocked Kira's small, lifeless body and reached out to hold Kathy's hand. As the rain settled around them, the leaves floated down the river to meet Kira in some other place.

Chapter Eight
Mary's Song

They reached the camp shortly after. Kathy's screams and sobs arrived before they did. A group of worried faces greeted them outside the ring of caravans. Heath carried Kira's small body. Mary came running forward, crying and fighting to hold the child. As they walked through the crowd of Travellers, Kathy felt hands reach out to touch her arm or squeeze her shoulders to console her. Someone wrapped Kathy in a wool blanket but, despite its warmth, it didn't stop her from shaking uncontrollably. Mary cried out in pain. When Kathy looked back, she found her kneeling on the grass, rocking Kira's still body while sobbing into her wet hair.

Kathy wasn't sure who was leading her into the camp, but she didn't care. She followed their pull on her arm as she stared blankly around her. She found Heath next to Cian. Sloane was squeezing him tight and pushing his hair back, relieved that the body wasn't his. It was only when Kathy reached the very old door with the black cat perched on the porch that she knew where she was. Laoise moved in front of Kathy to unlock the door with an old key from her pocket. She led Kathy into the incensed air and beaconed her to take a seat near the cast-iron stove.

The warmth from the stove started to bring Kathy's

limbs back to life. She stretched her fingers close to the cast-iron door. She felt the heat pierce her frozen joints. Kathy gazed over the room. Laoise was adding some leaves and dark, dried berries into the tin kettle before setting it on top of the stove. She didn't speak while they waited for it to boil. Instead, she moved around her caravan, pulling jars from the shelves that lined the interior of the room. She emptied their contents into a stone bowl and began to crush the ingredients with a pistol. When the kettle had boiled, Laoise moved her body slowly to the stove and picked up the hot handle with her bare hands. She poured the contents into two china cups on the table, sliding one to Kathy.

"Drink this," she said softly.

Kathy wrapped her hands around the thin china and stared down at the dark liquid. It smelled of peppermint with a tinge of something tart. Laoise brought the cup to her thin lips and took a small sip before returning it to her saucer.

"It's elderberry and peppermint. It'll help calm the nerves."

Kathy studied the dark liquid before bringing it to her mouth. Slowly, she drank from the cup and felt the hot liquid warm her body.

"Tell me what happened," Laoise said finally, resting her empty cup on the small table between them. She leaned back into the chair and folded her ringed hands on her lap. Kathy's eyes started to swell with tears. She took a sip of tea and sighed. She peered up at Laoise, who was patiently watching Kathy through her turquoise framed spectacles. Staring down at her cup, Kathy retold the story of how Kira wanted to collect leaves, how the wind and rain picked up suddenly and Kira ran away. How Kathy was so close to catching up with her, but she heard the voice of her friend calling to her from the trees.

Laoise nodded her head and waited until Kathy finished retelling the events before speaking again.

"She was taken by the good people," Laoise explained gravely, picking up the china cup and plate. "There was nothing you could have done to save her, Kathy. From the first time we found her we knew she was touched by them. But no matter how much foxglove we used, we couldn't get the fairy out of her." Laoise brought her ringed hands to her face. She pulled the spectacles from her small face and massaged the bridge of her nose.

"But she was right there, in front of me. If I had kept my eyes on her, she never would have ran off so quickly." Kathy buried her face in her own hands and wept.

Laoise reached out and placed a hand on Kathy's knee. "Hush child, there was nothing you could have done to save the girl. They can only take the ones who want to leave." Laoise heaved a heavy, chesty cough into an old handkerchief. She closed her eyes and leaned back in her armchair, while Kathy tried to muffle her sobs.

"You should clear your items from the caravan. We need to burn it by sunset," Laoise said simply, pulling her body up by the old velvet arms of the chair. She walked over to her counter and emptied the fine powder from the stone bowl into a glass bottle. She poured the rest of the contents from the kettle into the bottle before replacing the stopper.

"Will you bring this to Mary for me?" Laoise asked, passing Kathy the warm bottle. Kathy dried her eyes and took the bottle into her hand. She moved across the caravan to the door and pulled it open to reveal a late afternoon sun shining in.

"And Kathy, you mustn't take anything of Kira's Everything needs to be burned."

Kathy nodded stiffly before closing the old door behind her.

Kathy walked through the camp, searching for Mary. She heard the screaming and sobbing before she saw Mary's caravan. Kathy approached it, tentatively, and with a small hand she knocked on the painted wooden door. A few seconds later it was thrown open, revealing Tommy on the other side.

"This ain't a good time," he said, peering over his shoulder.

"Laoise asked me to deliver this to Mary," Kathy said quietly, passing Tommy the glass bottle. He took the bottle and nodded his head.

"Tommy... who's there?" Mary called from behind, pushing him aside.

"What have you done Kathy?" she cried. "I asked you to take care of her! Why did you let them take her?" she shouted, shaking Kathy by the shoulders.

Tommy pulled Mary back, making Kathy stumble on the steps and onto the ground.

"That's enough now Mary. Sure this isn't Kathy's fault!"

Tommy held Mary as she screamed and shouted. Her hands reached out to grab Kathy again. Mary tried to leave the caravan but Tommy pushed her inside.

"Leave now Kathy!" Tommy shouted, kicking the door closed with his boot. The caravan rocked as Kathy's entire body shook. She listened to the screams and shouting and the sound of china breaking. Footsteps crunched the ground next to her and she glanced down to see a pair of brown shoes.

"Come with me."

Kathy gazed up to see a hand in front of her. Her fingers wrapped around it and she felt the warmth fill her own cold palm. When she was pulled up from the wet ground she saw that the hand belonged to Birgitta. She held Kathy's red wool jumper in her arms and slowly unfolded it. Birgitta brought the red wool above Kathy's head and she lifted her arms to feel the warmth fall around her body. She hugged the wool as Birgitta wrapped an arm around her shoulders and walked her to their caravan. When they arrived, Fallon and Moira were busy filling a small wooden box with their items. Their mattresses, pillows and blankets lay on the ground. Birgitta walked Kathy up the steps. She positioned Kathy in front of the small bed that belonged to her and Kira and pulled out an old rucksack from underneath.

"Is this yours?" Birgitta asked, opening the top of the bag that revealed two books.

Kathy nodded slowly, looking around the bare

caravan. The wood stove had been turned off, its fuel and embers removed. The possessions that once filled the interior, like socks and stockings, were now packed away.

"What about this?" Birgitta asked, holding up the wooden box of leaves that belonged to Kira.

Kathy felt her throat tighten. "Yes," she whispered

Birgitta shoved the box inside Kathy's bag before closing it.

"Let's go," Birgitta said, as she carried the rucksack outside the caravan with Kathy at her side. Kathy looked back into the room and noticed a small pair of black shoes that belonged to Kira.

"But what about Kira's things?" she asked weakly. Birgitta held Kathy's arm and walked her over to where Fallon and Moira were sitting on a mattress on the ground.

"They need to stay in the caravan," Birgitta explained, dropping Kathy's bag next to the mattress.

"Here they come," Fallon whispered. Her eyes widened at the scene behind Kathy. A procession of men were walking in line to their caravan. Paddy and Cian were at the front, carrying a small body wrapped in burlap, with Kieran and Heath walking the tawny horse behind them. Mary stood to the side and was being held by Courtney. Bree stood next to them with Laoise.

Paddy and Cian carried the small body into the caravan, while Heath and Kieran saddled the horse to the wagon. Kathy felt the small squeeze of Birgitta's hand against her own as Paddy and Cian walked out of the caravan, leaving Kira's body inside. Both men climbed up onto the driver's bench. Heath passed them a metal canister before they beckoned the horse forward. The caravan jutted and moved from the circle. Mary ran to where the wheels had made small impressions into the grass and pulled at the ground crying and screaming. Courtney bent to her knees and comforted the convulsing woman.

Paddy and Cian continued to beckon the horse into the field, closer to the fairy fort than they ever dared to go before. Birgitta let go of Kathy's hand as Heath approached them. Fallon and Moira had already stood up from the mattress and were walking toward their old caravan. Heath took Kathy's hand and they walked into the field together. In the distance, Paddy unhitched the horse and walked her off to the side. Cian entered the caravan with the metal canister. When he emerged, he continued to splash the contents of the canister over the exterior, and then tossed it through the door which he shut before wiping his hands on his trousers. Kathy glanced up at the sun that had started to set. It was now hiding behind the fairy fort and left a ring of crimson around the trees. The whole sky was bright red, spilling over the rolling hills that lay beyond their field. A flicker of flame caught Kathy's eye and quickly their caravan was consumed by bright reds and yellows.

Mary sank to her knees and dug her fingers into the marshy, wet ground. She bowed her head on the grass and moaned. Heath wrapped his arms around Kathy, she hid her face into the nape of his neck. They heard the fire break the wood and spark. The smell of gasoline and burning flesh filled her nostrils. Kathy felt a wave of nausea hit her and she pulled away from Heath to bend over and throw up the contents of her empty stomach. She felt Heath's hands hold her hair and rub her back. Kathy felt her knees shake as she tried to pull herself up from her bent position. When Kathy stood, Birgitta and the other girls had started to walk back to camp. It was just Mary left, digging her nails deeper into the earth as she sobbed, while Heath and Kathy stood behind her. The wind started to howl and crackle from the fire. Kathy closed her eyes and heard a soft, trembling voice sing. Kathy walked up to Mary and knelt next to her on the grass. She reached out to hold Mary's hand and squeezed it, while she listened to Mary's song.

Heath gently pulled Kathy away from where she was sitting. "It's time to go now, Kath. We need to let her rest in peace."

Kathy followed Heath back to the line of caravans and wagons that were waiting to leave. The horses were impatiently pawing the ground. Tommy gave them a short nod as he walked past Heath and Kathy. He wrapped a black shawl around Mary's shoulders and picked her up as if she were just a child. Mary kept singing her song over and over again as if it were a prayer.

When they reached their wagon, Kathy saw the other girls and Braden sitting closely next to one another, next to their possessions. Heath helped Kathy over the wagon's side and together they huddled in the corner. Kathy dug her hands in her pocket and pulled out the small carved stone Kira had given her that morning. She held it in her palms and bowed her forehead to it. She felt the cold etching against her brow. The wagon pulled them onto the country lane and followed the procession of caravans. Kathy looked behind her. The darkness was swallowing the field and closing in on the small flame that held Kira's body while Mary's song carried them through the night.

Chapter Nine
The Story

They drove into the darkness, through dawn, and in late morning, they reached the town of Athlone. They watched the world drift by from the comfort of their wagon. The townspeople stood on the sidewalks, whispering while they rode past them. Kathy moved closer to Heath, who wrapped his arm around her body. Once they reached the edge of the town, they found a large green park next to a river. Kathy felt the jolt of the wagon as it moved them up the green mound. When they stopped, Heath opened the back latch and they all climbed out. Kathy stumbled when she jumped down. Heath grabbed her by the waist.

"It takes a while to get used to long journeys."

"Thanks," Kathy mumbled, picking her bag from the back and hoisting it over her shoulder.

Kieran walked over to Heath and gave him a pat on the shoulder. "Ready?" he asked.

Heath nodded. "I need to get some branches to make the tents."

"I'll come with you, I need to do something," Kathy said before pulling the bag off her shoulder and placing the carved stone inside it. She dropped the rucksack lightly on the pile of items Birgitta and Moira had already made. Kathy felt the damp from the grass chill her ankles as they walked down to the river where a small wood lay next to it. She hugged her jumper close to her body. Her head felt heavy from the night. It was cold and uncomfortable in the wagon and she didn't get much sleep. She just kept thinking of Kira's small body in the water. Kathy shuddered at the thought and walked faster to catch up to Heath and Kieran. Heath wrapped his arm around her as they went into the woods while Kieran hung back.

"We should wait until morning before leaving," he said, squeezing her closer. Kathy nodded and leaned her head against his shoulder.

"I can't believe she's gone, it just doesn't feel real." Heath leaned his chin against the top of her head.

"We'll get through this together, don't worry." Heath pulled her into a warm embrace and they stood like that for what felt like an eternity, listening to the leaves rustle around them.

***

It didn't take them long to find enough branches to build the two bender tents. Kieran stacked them just outside the woods on the field as Kathy and Heath searched for a few more. Kathy listened to the morning birds. She smelt the wet air. When she gazed up she could see the sun hitting the leaves on the tops of the trees.

"Ach!" Heath gasped, bent over, clutching his side.

Kathy ran up next to him. "Are you okay?"

He nodded and tried to stand straight. "I'm fine," he grimaced, his face pale.

"You don't look great. Why don't you sit for a

minute?" Kathy walked him over to a tree stump. Heath took a seat and immediately buried his face in his hands. Kathy brought the palm of her hand to his forehead and felt heat radiating from under his dishevelled hair.

"You have a fever; we should get you back to the camp." Heath shook his head and moved his hair from his eyes.

"It's not a big deal," he said, wincing and moving his hands to his side again.

"I'm going to get Kieran, he'll help me walk you back. Stay here." Kathy turned and jogged to the edge of the woods where she found Kieran by the pile of branches.

"You alright?"

Kathy shook her head. "It's Heath, something's wrong. He's gone all pale and he has fever. Can you help me walk him back to the camp?"

Kieran nodded and followed Kathy back to where she had left Heath. When they arrived, they found him on the ground, curled up on his side, moaning.

"Heath!" Kathy shouted, running towards him. She knelt beside him and moved the hair from his eyes. "You'll be okay, we're bringing you back to camp."

Kieran walked over and together they picked him up.

"Argh!" he cried, wincing and holding his side. Kieran ducked under his arm and propped him up against his body. Kathy did the same. They walked him through the woods as he moaned with pain. His face becoming paler as they did. When they reached the camp, the caravans had already been moved into their spiral shape.

"Go fetch Cian. I'll hold on to him," Kieran said as he held up Heath who looked like he was ready to faint.

Kathy ran through the caravans and to the centre fire. She looked frantically around her but couldn't find Cian. She walked along the caravans until she found the one painted yellow and impatiently knocked on the door. Sloane pulled the door open and stared down at her.

"What do you want?" she snapped. Kathy panted and pointed to the side of the caravans where Heath and Kieran were.

"It's Heath, he's sick. We need Cian to carry him." Sloane's face dropped. She turned, and shouted,

"Cian, get up, it's Heath!"

Kathy heard Cian move through the caravan and walk behind Sloane. "It's Heath, he's not well. Can you carry him?"

Cian nodded and followed Kathy.

"Bring him back here, I'll get Laoise!" Sloane added as they walked away.

Kathy led Cian to where Kieran was holding Heath up. In just that short time, Heath was looking worse. His skin was white with beads of sweat running down his forehead. He continued to moan as he held the side of his stomach in agony. Kathy's heart quickened, she'd seen this before. She remembered the outbreak that happened in the orphanage just a few winters ago. More than half the girls were in their beds for months.

Half of them survived, the other half didn't. Kathy rushed over and touched his arm. She drew her hand to his forehead and glanced desperately up at Cian.

"He's burning up."

Cian nodded, and with Kieran's help, picked Heath up in his arms.

Heath looked so small; this young man who held her through the cold night and comforted her from yesterday's tragedy was no more than a frail, whimpering boy in the arms of his guardian. Cian walked Heath through the gap between two caravans to his own, where Sloane waited anxiously.

She held the hem of her dress tightly, making her knuckles match the shade of Heath's face. Cian walked past her into the caravan carrying Heath.

"Heath!" Sloane cried, running up to touch his hot face. "What happened?" she shouted, looking at Kathy and Kieran.

"We were just in the woods gathering sticks and he became really pale and started to clutch his stomach."

"Laoise, thank God you're here. He's inside," Sloane said, stepping back from the door. Laoise climbed up the steps, clutching the front of her dress that held an assortment of glass bottles.

Kathy stepped toward the caravan but Sloane quickly blocked the door.

"You're not going anywhere near him," she snarled, pointing her finger at Kathy's chest. "You did this! First Kira and now Heath. You're cursed," she exclaimed, spitting at Kathy's feet. Kathy stumbled back into Kieran.

"C'mon Kathy," Kieran said gently, taking her arm and walking her toward the centre fire. "There's nothing we can do for him now, we just need to wait."

***

The following weeks were the longest of Kathy's life. She had spent her nights wide awake, staring up at the canvas ceiling of their tent, listening to the slow breathing next to her. Kathy had kept Kira's box of leaves under her pillow. She'd reach underneath and her hand would feel the smooth wood against her fingers. She tried to sleep but whenever she closed her eyes, images of Kira's little body floating in the reeds came back to her again and again.

In the early mornings, when the girls were still sleeping, Kathy would creep out of the tent and carefully open the box of leaves. She'd lift each leaf up to the rising sun. The red from the sunlight would pour around the leaf like it was floating in fire. When the sun turned yellow, Kathy would creep back into the tent and return the box under her pillow. She'd spend the rest of her day walking around the camp for hours on end. If it weren't for the food Kieran brought her at different intervals, she wouldn't have eaten anything. Each time he'd approach, she'd stop in her tracks and look up eagerly. He'd shake his head to let her know there was no change and leave her bowl on the grass. She'd drop to the ground and sob, hugging her knees close to her chest. And when she ran out of tears she would sit up again, eat the food on her plate and continue to walk around the camp until it became too dark to see the grass ahead of her.

One morning, Kathy sensed something changed.

She was lying on her back drifting in and out of an in-between sleep. It was dark but the birds had started to sing so she knew it was dawn. Her eyes opened wide when she heard voices near the tent. She heard Cian whispering, with what sounded like Paddy, in hushed voices. Kathy stood up and crawled closer to the edge of the tent.

"I don't like the look of her," Paddy said.

"Ay but Heath is only gettin' worse. Laoise said the fairy doctor is our only choice." She heard him say before he heaved a sigh.

"He'll come through; he's a strong lad our Heath."

"Ay, I hope you're right."

The voices got softer and farther away. Kathy scrambled to the end of the mattress she was sharing with Birgitta and found her dress. She dropped the dark wool over her messy hair and pulled on her stockings up to her knees. She stepped into her shoes and quickly walked out of the tent as the other girls slept peacefully into the dawn. Kathy shivered as she stepped into the misty morning. A light fog rested on the grass around her. She gazed up at the sky that was somewhere between day and night, the edges around it were growing into a warm purple light.

Kathy crept to Sloane's caravan. She found the door wide open, with Cian and Paddy standing outside, nervously talking in hushed voices with their hands in their pockets. Candles and gas lamps were lit which illuminated the interior and spilled out onto the wet, foggy grass. Kathy carefully walked behind the caravan and found a window on the far side, covered by a light curtain. She could make out the shadow of a body wrapped in blankets, stirring back and forth. Kathy's heart broke when she discovered it was Heath. Sloane held his hand and glanced up at an old woman dressed in black. Kathy studied the old woman as she walked out of the caravan and to the fire. She followed her there, and while hiding near the side of another caravan, she watched the old woman kneel on the soft ground. Her long grey hair touched the dirt behind her. From her pocket, the woman drew three small stems and placed them on a hot stone near the white coals whispering, "For the stroke, for the wind, for the evil eye."

The old woman pulled from her pockets a small silver bowl and a glass bottle with clear liquid. Kathy watched as she removed the glass stopper and poured the clear liquid into the dish, her face lifted to the rising sun, chanting. After the stems had turned black from the fire, she picked them up with her sagging fingers and dropped them into the dish of clear liquid. She bowed her head and lifted a stem from the water before whispering to the sun. With her other hand, she removed the remaining stems and threw them into the fire. Her small palm closed over the last wet stem. She moved the empty bottle underneath her hand and ground the stem between her fingers into the bottle. The old woman poured the clear liquid from the bowl into the bottle before returning the stopper. She held it with both hands and began to chant. The language was unfamiliar to Kathy and she began to feel uncomfortable. As if she was witnessing something she shouldn't have been watching. After a few minutes, the woman dressed in black finally stood. Kathy watched her gesture someone to the fire. Sloane and Laoise approached her.

"He's been touched by the good people," the woman said simply. Her hands held the bottle lightly. Sloane dropped to her knees and cried. Laoise brought her ringed hand to Sloane's bright red hair and stroked it gently.

"We lost a changeling at Ballycarrol Caher."

The woman drew in a sharp breath and stepped back.

"Did you burn everything?" she asked quietly. Laoise removed her turquoise spectacles and brought a ringed hand to the bridge of her nose. "Yes, we burned the caravan and all of the girl's possessions."

The woman in black shook her head. "They're angry about something."

Laoise replaced her turquoise spectacles before looking down at Sloane, who was sobbing on the ground.

"Is there anything you can do for him?"

The woman thought about this for a minute looking down at Sloane.

"He can take this potion here," she said, lifting the glass bottle. "But I'm afraid there's not much else we can do but wait to see what themselves have planned."
The three women walked back to Sloane's caravan.

Kathy felt her heart pound against her chest. She

remembered the box that was under her pillow. Kathy looked around. If she could get back to the tent and to the fire, before anyone saw her, she could burn it and everything would be set right again.

Kathy slipped through the caravans and ran across the camp to her tent. Kathy tried to calm her breathing as she climbed under the canvas and carefully tiptoed over to her mattress. She bent down and pulled the box of leaves from under her pillow. Birgitta rolled over and muttered something in her sleep before turning again. Kathy held the box close to her body and quietly walked out of the tent. She ran towards the centre fire but when she arrived Bree and Courtney were already making their morning bread. Kathy cursed under her breath. She peered down at the wooden box under her arms.

If she could just burn Kira's box then Heath would be healthy again. Kathy glanced around and spotted a packet of matches left on the porch of the bright blue caravan to her right. She walked over and avoiding any attention, pocketed the matches.

"Morning Kathy," Bree called, walking by as she wiped her hands on her apron.

Kathy turned quickly on her heel and moved the box and matches behind her back.

"M... morning Bree."

"Awful thing about Heath, isn't it? We're gonna make a nice chicken soup tonight. Courtney says there's nothing like a good chicken soup to break a fever."

Kathy looked around awkwardly. She peered

back to the tent as Birgitta and Fallon climbed out, stretching their arms and yawning.

"That's grand. I need to get back now."

Bree nodded sympathetically and brought her hand to Kathy's arm.

"Course, if you need anything, you just let me know."

Kathy nodded stiffly and backed away, forcing a small smile before disappearing between two caravans. Once outside of the camp, Kathy ran to the spot where Heath fell ill weeks ago. When she got to the woods, she found a clearing and made a pile of twigs and dried leaves. Feeling desperate, with her heart pounding, she swiped the first match and with a shaky hand brought its tiny flame to the tinder. They crinkled immediately and caught fire. Sure enough, the kindling started to spark and a small flame appeared.

Kathy sighed with relief and found a few branches to help raise the fire. Once it was ablaze, Kathy opened the wooden box. She paused for a moment, looking at the wild flame and took a deep breath. Kathy lifted the leaves from the box and tossed them into the flames. Her quiet sobs were drowned by the sounds of crackling, as the leaves were caught in the heat and quickly consumed.

Kathy was so angry with grief and fear. She was on her knees bent over and sobbing. She clutched the wooden box achingly as the last few leaves were slowly burned into nothing but smoke and dust. After wiping her eyes quickly she threw the box into the flames with such a force it made the fire hiss and caused some of the twigs to roll out of the pile, as if it angrily spat back at Kathy. The flames licked the wood eagerly. Kathy stared back up to the direction of the camp and silently prayed to herself that this would be enough to please the good people.

Once the fire consumed everything, and all that was left were bits of charcoal, Kathy threw dirt onto the fire to extinguish it. When the fire was out, she quickly walked up to the camp to check on Heath. As Kathy approached Sloane's caravan, she spotted Birgitta whispering to Braden. Birgitta looked over to Kathy as she walked up to them. She had a grave look on her face. Kathy's pace quickened, her heart pounding harder as she got nearer.

"It's not looking good, Kathy," Birgitta said quietly. She twisted a piece of her long blonde hair nervously. "They don't think he's going to make it." Her voice broke as she stared down at her feet.

Kathy shook her head and pushed past Braden and Birgitta. That couldn't be true, she thought to herself. She had burned the box of leaves so everything would be fine. He would get better now. She rushed through the camp to where the yellow painted caravan stood. Cian was outside, slouched in a chair. When Kathy approached the door he stood up and moved in front of her.

"Easy there, I don't think it's best for you to go in."

Kathy pushed against him, she felt a rage burn inside her belly.

"You can't stop me!" she yelled. "Heath, Heath can you hear me? I'm sorry, I'm sorry but you need to hang on." She pushed against Cian's stone, hard body, his arm holding her back.

"Let me through," she hissed.

"What's going on here?" Kathy turned her head and saw Laoise watching her struggle against Cian to get inside the caravan. Laoise held a glass bottle in her hand and a look of disappointment ran across her eyes when she focused on Cian.

"Kathy, help me administer this to Heath," Laoise said simply. Cian brought his hand to his neck and stepped back from the door, returning to his seat as he mumbled, "Sloane won't like this."

Kathy walked up the steps behind Laoise. She heard in the distance Sloane asking why Kathy was there but the only thing that mattered was a frail body wrapped in blankets on the bed. His skin was colourless, his hair was wet and stuck to his forehead. Kathy rushed over and knelt next to him. She grabbed his hand and squeezed it lightly to let him know she was there. He stirred in his sleep, his eyes flickered and then opened. He smiled and whispered a strained, "Kath," before closing his eyes again, while his head rolled to one side. Laoise gently placed a hand on Kathy's shoulder.

"I just need him to drink this, it will help."

Kathy nodded and backed away slowly as Laoise brought a ringed hand against his clammy forehead. She poured a bit of the liquid into a silver spoon and dripped it carefully into his mouth. Kathy felt fear grip her heart.

"Will he be okay?" she croaked, looking up at Laoise who stared back through her turquoise spectacles.

"There is a chance he can break the fever today," she said gravely. "Why don't you stay a while with him? He enjoys your company and that will help him recover," she suggested, casting a look at Sloane. "Sloane, you can help me collect some more elderberries. He could use another dose in a few hours."

"But..."

"It's the best way you can help Heath right now," she said gently, placing her ringed hand on Sloane's arm and leading her out of the caravan. Sloane studied Kathy before turning and following Laoise outside.

Kathy reached out her hand and stroked Heath's wet forehead. His skin burned against hers. She gazed at his pale face. He looked dead lying on that bed; his small body wrapped in wool blankets. Kathy climbed into bed next to him and laid her hand on his chest. She felt it rise with every small breath he took. She listened to the noises coming from outside the caravan. The background of people talking, the gusts of wind that knocked against the stained glass windows. As she stroked his hand, the colour from the stained glass started to dance on the caravan floor. They looked like birds flying and it reminded her of a story she had read in The Book of Moons.

She told Heath the story of the beautiful, great birds Émer, the wife of Cú Chulainn, saw one day. And how she boasted that her husband could catch one for every woman in their village. But when he tried to catch a bird for his wife he failed because it was actually a goddess named Fand. The goddess was angry and gave him an illness but then she fell in love with Cú Chulainn. Though she wanted to take him for his lover, Émer's love for her husband was more than Fand's. And when this was proved, Fand gave back Émer's husband and they lived happily ever after.

After she finished telling the story Kathy fell asleep. She woke up hours later in the middle of the night. Her eyes were tired. She squinted in the dark and saw Sloane's silhouette fast asleep on an armchair near the cast-iron stove. Her legs were curled up to her chest, while her hair flowed down the back of the chair. Kathy saw the light from the fire dance across her tired face.

Kathy glanced down at Heath, noticing his breathing was becoming steadier.

"I love you, Heath," Kathy whispered, placing her head on his chest, listening for his heartbeat which was now beating fast and strong. She stroked the skin of his chest before reaching behind her neck and unclasping the Celtic cross necklace. Kathy tied it around Heath's neck. She held the cross between her fingers as his stomach gently rose and fell again. She grabbed his hand and held it tightly. She prayed that he would be safe now that Kira's box was destroyed.

In her heart, she felt a kind of loneliness she hadn't felt in a long time. She felt it fill her chest and stomach as she thought of the empty days and nights she spent in the orphanage. How Sinead and Kathy would watch their classmates, just before Christmas break, talk about all the presents they were going to get from their families. About their grandmothers' houses they would walk to after school for biscuits and tea. On those days, they would take the long way back to Ennis Orphanage. They'd walk along the River Fergus and imagine a world they would never have. They'd talk about the presents they'd get that year from their parents. What biscuits their grandmothers' would lay out for them. Sinead would explain how her father would always leave Christmas shopping to the last minute. How he'd rush out on Christmas Eve to buy a mountain of gifts just before the shops closed. Kathy would say her mother would lay out a new dress with matching stockings and a hair piece for her to wear Christmas morning.

They talked about how they'd both sneak out before their family meals and tell each other what they opened that morning before returning home. That the door would open, her mother would give her a look of amused disappointment and order her to clean her hands before she sat down to eat. And when Kathy laid her head on her tiny bed in the damp room, she imagined it was against her father's shoulder in a warm lounge, with the heat of the fire dancing behind her eyes. As she clutched her hungry belly, she imagined her stomach was full from supper and laughter earlier that day. And in those comforts she would drift into a dream that could have been in either reality.

***

Kathy felt a soft squeeze on her hand, and when she opened her eyes she saw Heath awake looking down at her. The early morning light poured on his face and revealed a healthy flush on his cheeks.

"Hi," he whispered weakly, placing his hand on her head and stroking her hair. Kathy looked up and smiled.

"Hi," she croaked through a sob.

"I'm not going anywhere," he whispered, pulling her in close and holding her against his chest. Kathy cried with relief into his shirt as he stroked her hair and gently kissed her forehead.

"Why don't you tell me another story?"

Kathy wiped her eyes with her hands. "You remember that?"

He nodded and smiled. "Your voice is soothing."

"Okay," she said, sniffing and wiping her cheeks. "Okay, there's one about a poet's curse, of the great chief poet of Ireland, Dallán Forgaill, who was proud and had a quick temper. And how one evening he was challenged by Mongán, the prince." Kathy told Heath the story of how the poet was so upset about being challenged that he said he would curse the land unless the prince would give up his wife. But in the end the prince was able to prove he was right, when a ghost appeared to confirm the story. So the poet bitterly admitted his defeat and snuck out of the court like a wounded dog, without ever cursing Ulster.

Heath laughed. "Poets have a nasty temper, don't they?"

Kathy chuckled, peered over and noticed Sloane was watching from her armchair.

"That was my father's favourite story. He tried to tell it to me but said he could never remember the words." Sloane stood up from her armchair and pulled the shawl around her shoulders closer to her body.

"Where did you learn that story?"

Kathy looked up at Heath, who was no longer smiling. "I... I just heard it from somewhere before."

Sloane approached them. Kathy moved herself from underneath Heath's arm to sit up. Sloane reached out and placed her hand on top of Heath's forehead.

"Your fever's broken," she said to Heath in disbelief. "I need to find Laoise." She backed away slowly, turning around to look at them both again before leaving the caravan. Kathy stood up quickly and ran her hands through her hair.

"This is bad, Heath."

"What do you mean?" Heath asked, sliding up the bed, attempting to sit up with the support of his pillows.

"If Sloane tells Laoise about the story I just told, she'll know I stole The Book of Moons from her!"

Heath groaned and moved his hair back from his face.

"Jesus, Kath, I told you not to read that thing!"

"It was your idea that I pretend to be a storyteller in Dublin," Kathy hissed, crossing her arms. "What are we going to do? What if she kicks me out? You're not strong enough to go anywhere."

"Just relax, Kath. No one's goin' anywhere. For all we know, Sloane is getting Laoise to bring some kind of herb." He leaned his head against the wood panelling of the caravan. "Besides, she likes you."

Kathy sat at the edge of the bed and held her

forehead in her hands.

"I don't want to leave you Heath," she said, looking up at him. Heath reached out and stroked her hair that fell along her back.

"You won't."

The caravan door opened and Laoise walked in with a few glass bottles in her hands. She gave Heath a weak smile as she brought her ringed hand to his forehead.

"Sloane's right, your fever has broken." She removed a stopper from the bottle with a dark purple syrup before passing it to him. "Now drink this and Sloane, pass me that kettle."

Sloane handed her the small tin kettle. Laoise poured the contents of the second glass bottle into the kettle before passing it back to her.

"Place it on the stove and let it boil. Heath, when it is ready, you're to drink the entire contents of it, understood?" Laoise asked as Heath grimaced while drinking the last few drops of the thick purple syrup. He nodded and wiped his mouth on his sleeve. Laoise turned to Kathy and stared at her through her large spectacles.

"I think it's time we leave Heath to rest some more. Come with me." Kathy looked back at Heath who squeezed her hand in reassurance.

"I'll see you later," he whispered. Sloane pushed Kathy aside to give Heath a steaming cup from the kettle. Kathy smiled weakly and followed Laoise to her caravan.

***

Kathy squinted at the morning sun that was shining brightly over the camp. She crossed her arms close to her body while following Laoise past the centre fire and to her caravan. The old woman walked up the steps, past the black cat that was sleeping soundly in a small ball. She pulled a key from her pocket and unlatched the lock. When she opened the door, the cat stretched its front legs and walked inside. Kathy walked up the steps and into the caravan. Laoise poured milk into a small dish before setting it on the ground. The cat immediately went to the milk and started to drink it noisily in the corner.

"I'm sorry Laoise," Kathy said, crossing her arms tightly around her waist. "I took The Book of Moons from your chest... that's how I know the story," Kathy explained, looking down at her feet. "I never should have done it. And I should have brought it right back. I've kept it safe. I can get it for you now?" Kathy asked. Her heart pounded against her chest as she imagined what kind of punishment Laoise would give her. Would they leave her here by herself? Would they no longer feed her?

Laoise sat down slowly on the armchair next to her cast-iron stove and gestured for Kathy to sit next to her. She pulled her spectacles off and rubbed the sides of her nose. When she returned them to her face she studied Kathy with her light blue eyes.

"They're not my books," Laoise replied simply, reaching for the kettle that was boiling on top of the stove. She poured some tea into two mugs and passed Kathy one.

"I've had them for a long time but they were never mine. I've just been looking after them for a very old friend." She poured some milk into her cup and offered Kathy some.

"Am I in trouble?" Kathy asked.

Laoise shook her head. "No, not with me, anyway." Kathy leaned back into her chair and took a long sip from her tea cup. "Heath said it was given to a storyteller from the fairies, is that true?"

"Yes, or at least that's how the story goes. The first storyteller in Ireland helped the High King with a very special mission. He had to go to the Otherworld to help him and time passes more slowly there, so what seemed like a night for the storyteller in the Otherworld turned out to be thirty years in our world. The High King gave the storyteller The Book of Moons, knowing this would happen. You see, it isn't just a book about stories. The book makes storytellers. Knowing that he only had a few hours left to live, the storyteller travelled to as many houses as he could, sharing The Book of Moons with each family as he went. He only managed to get to five families. The tradition of storytelling stayed within those families but slowly they too started to disappear," Laoise explained, before taking a long sip from her cup as she leaned back.

"These families were important to us Travellers. The stories they wove formed the very fabric that kept us together. They told us who we were. They gave us a glimpse of things from the past so we could learn for the future." Laoise pulled out an old handkerchief from her sleeve and heaved a chesty cough into it. Kathy heard phlegm rattle in her lungs as she leaned forward.

"But where did they go?" Kathy asked quietly, looking down at her hands in her lap.

"It became harder for the storytellers to travel. Our clans had to get smaller. Ireland was breaking apart then and it wasn't safe for us Travellers to be seen. To this day, most Traveller clans are small. We're the last of this size."

"A few storytelling families left Ireland for America, they were searching for a better life, while others went to fight to free the country. Other families just stopped all together." Laoise stood and walked over to the old chest. She pulled a key from her pocket and unlocked the latch. She opened it slowly and from within it she drew a large leather-bound book that seemed older than the one Kathy had in her rucksack. Laoise walked over to her chair and sat down again.

She looked at Kathy with her blue eyes.

"You have a choice now Kathy. You're the only one in the world who's seen The Book of Moons. You've been given the power to read these books." Laoise handed her the large book.

Kathy felt the weight of it in her hands and the smooth leather against her fingers. "But I didn't mean for it to happen. I never meant to become a storyteller."

"But it did happen, Kathy. The book doesn't appear to just anyone. It's been waiting in that chest for fifty years for the right person. You're the right person. You can choose to be the one that brings back storytelling."

"What if I get it wrong? What if I'm not ready?"

"They'll wait for you. They've already waited fifty years," Laoise said simply, finishing her tea.

Chapter Ten

The Storyteller

Kathy visited Heath after her meeting with Laoise and retold him what she had said. He listened as he propped himself up on some pillows, playing with the Celtic cross around his neck.

"So what are you going to do?" he asked when she finished retelling the story for him.

"I think I need to try, at least. Who knows when you'll be better to move." She noticed the dark circles under his eyes. His face was thin from weeks of eating very little.

"I'm sorry, Kath. If it weren't for me you'd be in Dublin by now."

Kathy picked up the cross around his neck and felt its points press into her fingertips.

"Sinead would understand, and it won't be long before you're strong enough to travel."

Heath moved his hands to unfasten the necklace around his neck but Kathy rested her hand on his arm.

"You should wear it, it'll keep you safe."

He picked up the Celtic cross for a better look. "Where did you get it?"

"Sinead gave it to me, it belonged to her sister. She said it protects people who wear it."

Heath lifted his wrist and unfastened the leather bracelet around it.

"Here," Heath said, passing it to Kathy. "What's this for?"

"It only seems fair that you wear something of mine." Heath reached over and wrapped the long leather band around her wrist twice before clasping it. "When I look down at it I think of the patience Cian must have had to work the leather like that." He stroked it with his finger which gently brushed against Kathy's wrist.

"How you can't force things with your own time. You need to wait till their ready." He moved his hand up her arm and gave it a small squeeze.

"We'll get to Dublin when we're meant to get there."

***

That evening, when Kathy returned to her tent, she found Moira, Fallon and Birgitta huddled together, whispering on a mattress in the corner. As she entered, they fell silent and watched Kathy cross the tent. When she turned to take off her clothes, they started to whisper again in hushed voices. Kathy felt a fire burn in her stomach. She turned and snapped, "Why don't you say it to my face?"

"What are you talking about?" Birgitta replied, stroking her blonde hair.

"Instead of just whispering behind my back, why don't you just say it to my face," Kathy said, crossing her arms.

Birgitta stood up. "Fine, we think you're nothing but trouble. Ever since you arrived everything's been awful. Kira's dead, Heath almost died. We broke down in front of a fort. It's all your fault!"

"Why would it matter to you?" Kathy shouted back. "You never cared for Heath and you certainly never cared about Kira. You all thought she was a changeling and never even looked at her!"

Birgitta's eyes started to swell with tears. "Just go away; you don't belong here!"

Kathy ran out of the tent. She felt a wave of guilt. She knew it was her fault Kira died. If she hadn't seen Sinead in the trees that day, she would have caught Kira before she got to the river. Kathy didn't need reminding of how terrible she'd made things. She crossed her arms and hugged her dress closer to her body. Kathy walked around the circle of the camp, thinking of where she could sleep. Her body felt tired from watching over Heath the night before. She raised her face to the sky and felt the soft drops of water against her skin. It was too wet and cold to sleep outside. She turned and walked through a pair of caravans in the direction of the horses. She would take Heath's bed.

"Can I come in?" Kathy asked, standing in the entrance of the boy's tent. Kieran nodded, while he sat cross legged on his bed carving a stick. Kathy walked into the tent and moved closer to the small fire in the centre. Braden sat on a crate next to it, shirtless and lifting weights. Kathy averted her eyes and blushed.

"Hey," she said awkwardly. Braden nodded before returning to his weights.

"Would you mind if I stayed here tonight?" Kathy

asked, looking at Kieran.

"Sure, Heath's bed is behind you."

Kathy mumbled a thanks before taking off her shoes and crawling under the quilts. It was warm and soft, and smelled like Heath. The mix of his musk and dirt was comforting. Kathy listened to the soft pattering of rain against the fabric of the tent before drifting into the night.

***

When she opened her eyes, Kathy was no longer in the tent with Kieran and Braden. Instead, she was in a circular, stone room. Each side of the room had a different archway leading from the circle. A large oak tree grew from the stone centre and reached to the ceiling. Kathy walked around the room and peered into the different openings; each one leading to a different garden. Kathy listened to the sound her shoes made against the stone floor. It sounded like her footsteps in the orphanage.

Kathy stopped in front of one archway. She peered into the garden but it was too bright to see anything except for an overgrown path lined with flower beds on either side. Kathy stepped out onto the path and felt the softness of the moss covered stones beneath her feet. She followed the path to a set of stone steps. She climbed them and found herself in an enclosed clearing, lined with sycamore trees. In the centre was a pond with a little girl kneeling next to it, poking the still water with a stick. Kathy walked closer and saw she had long dark hair like Kira's.

"Kira!" Kathy exclaimed, running towards her.

The little girl turned to face Kathy. Kathy gave her a hug but the child pulled away. From behind her back she pulled out a large leather-bound book which she handed to Kathy.

"Will you read me a story?" she asked in a small voice, sitting cross-legged by the edge of the pond. Kathy sat down next to her and opened the book. She stared at the pages but the words were too blurry for her to read them.

"I'm sorry, I can't read this."

Kathy glanced next to her but the little girl was gone.

"Kira, where are you?" Kathy called, looking around at the empty clearing. Kathy gazed into the pond. Sycamore leaves were landing softly on its surface, making small ripples across the water. Kathy peered back at the book on her lap and picked the leaves from its pages. The words were coming into focus.

"Kira, come back! I can read it now! I can read you the story!"

"Kathy?" a voice called.

Kathy jerked awake, her forehead damp with sweat. She squinted at the light shining through the opening of the tent. She sat up quickly and ran her hand through her auburn hair, inhaling deeply to catch her breath.

"Are you okay, Kathy?"

She looked up and found Kieran standing over her. "I-I'm fine."

"You were shouting Kira's name..."

"...it's nothing, forget about it."

"Okay. I saved you a bread roll from breakfast." Kathy sat up slowly and took the bread from Kieran's palm.

"Thanks," she mumbled, taking a bite from the bun. Her stomach growled, she hadn't eaten in over a day.

"You should probably check on Heath." Kieran said, lifting his hand to his head and scratching the dandruff from his hair.

"He's in a foul mood. He's been told he can't perform at the Midnight Circus."

"That's tonight?" Kathy asked, bread crumbs dropping from her mouth.

Kieran nodded. "Ay, and then off to Kells later, for the Samhain."

Kathy nodded and wiped her mouth on her sleeve. "Thanks, I better go see him."

Kieran followed her out of the tent and waved before walking back to the horses. Kathy felt the cool morning air caress her face. As she walked to the yellow painted caravan she tried to remember the dream that made her shout but it was quickly slipping from her mind.

***

"You shouldn't force yourself to get up," Kathy said, pushing Heath back down on the bed.

"It isn't right being locked up in here while the Midnight Circus is going on out there," Heath exclaimed, pulling back the curtain sharply. They both listened to the voices and laughter coming from the camp as non-Travellers from around the area started to pour in to catch glimpses of their talents.

Kathy laid back on her side and admired Sloane's caravan. She had taken to sneaking in at moments when she knew Cian and Sloane were busy.

"When do you think they'll move you back to your tent?" she asked. Heath folded his arms under his head and stared up at the ceiling.

"Soon, I hope. I can't stand Sloane fretting over me. She's convinced I'm going to run a fever at any moment."

Kathy moved a bit of hair from his forehead.

"It was scary, you know. I didn't think you were going to make it," she said quietly, thinking of the way he appeared on the bed. His body thin and pale, and the sweat that stuck to his skin and clung to his clothes. Kathy's grey-blue eyes surveyed him carefully. His colour was much better from the broth and bread Bree brought him every day but he was still thin from the weeks when he ate so little.

"I'm not going anywhere Kath," he said, reaching over to wrap his arm around her shoulder. Kathy waited until he fell asleep before she left. She crept through the dark caravan to the other end and opened the door. Sloane was on the other side, about to climb up the stairs. Kathy's body froze and she quickly averted her eyes.

"I was just leaving," Kathy mumbled, rushing past the woman.

"Kathy. Wait!" Sloane called, jogging to catch up. Kathy turned to face the red-headed woman, expecting an angry or disappointed look. She was surprised to find that Sloane seemed apologetic and embarrassed.

"I'm sorry for what I've said," Sloane explained, reaching out to touch Kathy's arm. Instinctively, Kathy backed away.

"I know I'm too protective of Heath, but I can't help it." Sloane's eyes started to water. "I've already lost one child and I can't lose another. He's all we have, our Heath," she sobbed, pulling out a handkerchief from her dress pocket.

"Traveller children are a rare breed and when you have them you have to hang on to them because you never know when they'll be taken from you." She blew her nose into the daisy patterned fabric.

Kathy felt sorry for the woman. Kathy felt a pang in her heart. She wanted to comfort her, to reach out and say she knew what it was like to lose someone but she couldn't find the words. Instead, Kathy stared down at her feet and kicked the dirt around her.

"I know we can't have him forever and that he's already a man. I know that he wants to go to Dublin with you but all I ask is that you wait until he's healthy enough to travel," Sloane pleaded, looking up from her handkerchief.

"Of course," Kathy mumbled.

Kathy walked away quickly, wrapping her arms around her body. She passed the last few visitors who were leaving the camp while the Travellers started to pack up the caravans.

Kathy found Kieran and Braden taking down their tent as Birgitta packed the blankets and mattresses into a wagon.

"This yours?" Kieran asked, picking up a small rucksack. Kathy nodded and mumbled a thanks before pulling the rucksack on her back.

"Need help?" she asked.

Kathy walked over and accepted a bundle of fabric from Kieran. She walked to the wagon and dropped it in, walking past Birgitta in the process who refused to look up at her.

"I'm going to help the others," Kathy said, walking away from the group. She walked through the camp, looking at everyone as they were packing and getting ready for a full night's journey. She thought about going to help Mary but she hadn't spoken to Kathy in the four weeks that had passed since Kira's death. She couldn't see Heath because he would be with Sloane and Cian. Kathy glanced around her, it seemed that everyone knew their place. They all had a job or something to do and they just got on with it. Kathy felt a pang of loneliness in her stomach as she walked through the camp. When they finished, she walked back to the wagon and climbed into it, clutching the rucksack against her chest. She avoided looking at Birgitta and Fallon, who were whispering again, and instead gazed out at the trees that surrounded them through the night.

***

Kathy held the red wool jumper close to her body as

the town of Kells unfolded around her. The fog on the road reached up to meet them. Kathy pulled her numb legs tightly to her, wishing Heath were here to hold her close and keep her warm. She peered up and saw a tall, narrow tower in the distance. They continued down the road until they reached a small field just outside of the town. Kathy thought of Sinead and wondered if she was still travelling to Dublin too. Did she meet someone in Ennis who could only take her as far as Kells? Maybe she was here, walking these streets. Or did she meet some people along the way? Kathy imagined Sinead laughing in the back of a car while two college students drove back to Trinity College. They'd share stories and when they reached Dublin she'd get out and ask them where the nearest hostel was and where she could get some work. Sinead was always the resourceful one. She knew what to ask and where to go. They'd give her their number and promise to meet up. And perhaps on a cold day like this day, she'd meet up for coffee with them.

Kathy felt the wagon climb a steep incline and grabbed the sides of it to steady herself. Braden stretched his arms above his head and yawned. Birgitta was brushing her hair while Fallon and Moira slept against each other. Kathy had been with these people for two months but nothing seemed familiar. The places were always changing and so were the people. Kathy's stomach turned when she thought of Kira. She longed to hold the girl's small hand in her own. To smell the familiar scent of her hair back in their caravan. She wished she could go back to that time but they kept moving forward, to new places.

When the camp was set up, Kathy walked over to Sloane's caravan. She felt lonely and wanted Heath's company. She peered through the curtains to see if anyone else was there with him. She saw Heath sitting up with Sloane and Cian. They were laughing and holding cups of tea. Cian reached over and patted Heath's back gently. A small crooked smile crept up on Heath's pale face. He appeared safe and happy sitting in that bed, covered with duvets and fluffy pillows.

Kathy felt a pain in her heart. She had always thought of Heath as an orphan like herself. But unlike her, he really had a family. He had people that would miss him when he'd leave. Could she really do that to him? Be the reason he loses his family? She hugged herself closer and walked away. The sky was grey now and soft water droplets were starting to fall. Most of the tents and caravans were already constructed and everyone had their place. She would leave the camp without Heath. Kathy walked over to where the horses were grazing the lush grass. She'd walk through Kells and find a ride to Dublin. She already had her bag on her back. She could leave now and no one would know she left.

Kathy walked through the camp, the rain pouring harder. She turned her face to the sky and felt it wash over her skin. She remembered the kiss they shared under rain just like this. Her hands moved to her lips as she imagined his soft tongue against hers. She glanced back at the caravan. A voice inside her was whispering to stay. Just for a little while longer, it said.

Could she leave him? Dublin was still miles away and the thought of being alone in a big city made Kathy feel small and hopeless. Maybe she didn't need to leave just yet.

Kathy turned and walked back to the centre of the camp. She walked up to the old caravan with its peeled paint and knocked softly on the door. Laoise pulled it open, clutching her shawl over her shoulders. "Come in," she offered, moving back into the room. Kathy followed her into the caravan and took a seat while

Laoise set the kettle on the stove.

"I've thought about what you said," Kathy began, pulling her knees to her chest, trying to keep her body small and warm next to the fire. "I'd like to try... if that's okay." Laoise smiled gently while she set cups down and picked up the boiling kettle.

"That's grand," she said, pouring some tea into Kathy's cup. Kathy added milk and held the steaming cup to her lips. She gazed over at the chest of books. Laoise followed her gaze.

"You could start now," Laoise suggested taking a seat at her small round table and leaving Kathy alone by the stove.

Kathy nodded and stood up. She walked over to the familiar chest and lifted the old wooden lid to release the dust. She looked down at her fingerprints that streaked the cover of a larger book that had been underneath the one she took all those months ago. Kathy gently picked it up and moved the dust off the cover. She peered over to Laoise who was busying herself by shuffling cards and spreading them out with her ringed fingers. Kathy closed the chest lid and walked back to her seat. She opened the cover and saw the book was written by hand. Kathy gently flipped through its yellowed pages. She noticed there were a few stories that had been written down multiple times in different handwriting.

"There's different versions of the same story in this one," Kathy said, looking up at Laoise. "How will I know which is the right one?"

Laoise glanced over at Kathy through her turquoise spectacles. "Find the one that feels right for you."

Kathy stared at the book and sighed.

***

While Heath continued to recover in the Sloane's caravan, Kathy returned to Laoises' each day to read the books. It had only been a week but Kathy had already read through the entire chest. To her frustration, all the books had multiple versions of the same stories. To make matters worse, each version had its own ending, or certain scenes removed or added. Kathy slammed a book closed one afternoon while Laoise was crushing some herbs.

"Sorry," Kathy mumbled, looking down at the book on her lap. "It's frustrating, I don't know which one is the real story." Laoise walked over and placed a ringed hand on her shoulder.

"They're all real."

"But how do I know which one to pick?" Kathy asked, burying her face in her hands. She thought of how foolish she'll look at the Midnight Circus. But she needed money to get to Dublin, especially since she couldn't rely on Heath. Kathy rubbed her eyes and looked up at Laoise who was watching her quietly. She sat down on the chair across from her.

"It's not about getting this perfect, Kathy. It's about learning to feel which story is right for what moment." Kathy studied the old leather on the book. It was faded and worn from being held many times before her.

"A great storyteller doesn't stick to one version of a story. A great storyteller knows their audience and knows what they need to hear in that moment."

"But isn't that lying?"

"The only truth people are looking for is their own. Sharing a story that's right for that moment will help them find their own truth."

"But how will I know if it's right?" Kathy asked, crossing her arms tightly around her chest.

Laoise reached out and touched her forearm.

"You knew the story Heath needed to hear when he was ill. And it gave him the courage to get through his illness. It didn't matter that there were fifty other versions of that story you could have told. You told him the one that came to you that night because that was the one he needed to hear." She leaned back against her armchair and removed her spectacles. She rubbed her tired eyes before setting them back on her long nose. "You don't need to do anything. Just be open to the story when it's the right time."

Kathy looked down at her lap and thought of that night with Heath. How she felt so scared and helpless. The story she shared helped her feel like she was doing something. She wanted to feel that again.

Laoise stacked her cards together, placing them at the edge of the table.

"It's time for coffee," she said gently, gesturing for Kathy to follow her out of the caravan. Laoise opened the door and stepped outside. Kathy followed and saw the group of Travellers gathered around the old caravan, waiting. She looked over at Birgitta who quickly averted her eyes. Heath stood back and gave her a small, crooked smile.

"I don't understand?" Kathy asked, looking up at Laoise who was still standing near the steps of her caravan.

"The word got out that you're a storyteller, Kathy." Kathy glanced up at Bree who was at the end of the crowd holding a steaming cup of coffee in her hand. She smiled and gestured for Kathy to collect it. Kathy peered back at Laoise who walked over and placed her hand on Kathy's back. She whispered in Kathy's ear, "The storyteller gets the first cup of coffee."

Laoise gave her a little push and Kathy tripped forward. She awkwardly walked through the crowd of people. The faces looking back at her seemed foreign. Bree stretched her shaky hand and offered her the mug. Kathy timidly lifted her own hands to take the cup. She listened as everyone held their breath. Kathy searched around and found Heath in the crowd. He gave her an encouraging nod. She lifted the cup to her lips and took a small sip of the earthy, velvet liquid that stung her tongue from its heat. She had never tasted the coffee so hot before. Heath and

Kathy always collected theirs at the very end and it was always filled with dregs from the bottom of the pot. When Kathy lifted her eyes from her cup she saw a sea of faces looking up at her. Their eyes wide with excitement and fear. Their storyteller had returned.

Chapter Eleven
Samhain

The nights grew longer as the weeks brought them closer to Samhain. Heath got stronger and finally left Sloane's caravan for the boy's tent. This made Kathy happy because it meant she could spend more time with him before leaving for Dublin by herself, after she had money from the Midnight Circus. It felt hard to be near him knowing that in only a few short days they would be apart. Heath didn't notice and spent most of his time practicing for the event to come. He said he felt rustier but Kathy thought his music sounded even more beautiful. It was as if the illness gave him a new rhythm he didn't have before.

On the day of Samhain, Kathy managed, with great difficulty, to retell the story she had shared with Kira all those months before; of the three children who got turned into swans from their jealous step mother. It wasn't perfect but it was enough to get her through the night.

Afterwards, Kathy continued to nervously pour over the different versions of that story. She tried to follow Laosie's advice on not thinking about which version of the story she should share. Kathy glanced up from her book and stared into the fire, from her peripheral vision she saw Courtney chop vegetables and throw them into a large pot. When she looked back to the fire she saw Mary approaching.

Kathy felt her throat tighten. She hadn't spoken to Mary since the day Kira drowned. She peered around her, Heath was practicing with Paddy at his caravan, the notes he played seemed far away. She studied the small package Mary was carrying in her arms.

"Kathy?" she asked timidly. Kathy glanced up from her book and gave her a small smile.

"I... I wanted you to have something special for tonight and the like. The girls always make something new for themselves on Samhain." She handed Kathy the small package tied with a string.

"Thank you," Kathy whispered, looking at her feet.

"I hope you like it, I think it's your colour."

Kathy nodded, looking down at her book. She wanted to stand up and give Mary a hug. She missed the comfort of her humming, the way her hands quickly tied and beaded the tiny string that made her bracelets. She wanted to tell her that she missed Kira too and wished she could go back to the way things were. Instead, she kept her head down and avoided her brown eyes.

"I'll leave you to your practicing and the like," Mary said quickly before turning and walking away. Kathy's shaking hand touched the soft, violet wool.

She untied the string and unrolled the package. It was a long sleeved, knitted dress. Mary had even added little jewels along the neckline. It was magical. Kathy held it to her nose and smelled the fabric. It reminded Kathy of Mary's caravan. She imagined Mary sitting in her wooden chair by the fire, knitting the dress while she hummed.

***

"I think I'm going to throw up."

"No you aren't. Just keep your head up. You'll do fine."

Kathy tried to raise her head as Heath suggested but she felt the blood drain from her face. She bent forward again.

"How am I going to say anything?"

Heath rubbed her back. "Don't worry, it'll go away soon enough. I felt terrible at my first performance too."

"Did it go okay?"

"Not really, I threw up on the lad next to me."

Kathy groaned and lifted herself up. She looked down at the violet knitted dress Mary had made her. She was thankful for the warm wool that shielded her from the damp night.

"Look, Laoise is gesturing for you to come forward."

"Oh God..."

"Go!' Heath whispered, giving Kathy a nudge so she stumbled next to Laoise. The other Travellers and settlers sat together in a semi-circle around the fire waiting for Kathy to speak. Laoise gave her a weak smile and walked over to the side where she could watch. She hunched over her handkerchief and coughed violently into it. Kathy looked away and stared into the fire. She closed her eyes and when she opened them she could see shapes starting to form in the flames.

She wanted to tell them about the children and the swans but the figures in the fire reminded her of something else. She glanced to her left where Laoise was sitting. She smiled and nodded. Kathy moved her eyes back to the flames. Her characters were forming themselves from the flames. They started to move, flickering with the sparks and dancing with the wind. Before she had time to think about it, her voice started to move with the images. Each word strung itself into the next and danced with the shapes as they flickered back at her in the light of the fire. These figures were more than alive, they burned with an intensity she had never seen before. Her eyes began to water and when she finally reached the end of the story, they faded into the ashes. She pressed a hand against her wet cheek. Everyone around the fire was standing and clapping in disbelief. She didn't look up at any of them. Kathy continued to stare at the bright embers where her characters had risen and fallen.

Heath walked over to her beaming, with his fiddle in one hand and a hat full of coins in the other.

"They loved you!" He lifted the hat to show her the pile of coins. Kathy moved her hand and held a few in her palm.

"It's yours, this is what people paid to hear you speak," Heath said.

Kathy stared down at the coins in her palm.

"You okay?" Heath asked, looking at her stunned face.

"I've never held money before," she said, looking up. Heath wrapped his arms around her shoulders and gave her a gentle squeeze.

"It sounds stupid," she said, wiping her eyes with her sleeves. "I just never had coins to go to the shop like all the other kids and now..." Her voice cracked as she pictured her and Sinead watching enviously as the other children went to the shop after school for sweets.

Heath wrapped his arm around her. "I know what this means to you, Kath. But you're more than all those kids and their pocket change combined. And this..." He gently closed her hand over the coins. "This could never amount to your true worth, no matter how much coin you might have. Remember that Kath," he said softly, pushing a wavy strand behind her ear.

"Thank you," she whispered, laying her head against his chest. She felt the worn cotton soft against her cheek. She inhaled and smiled, smelling the dance of musk, smoke and dirt that filled her nostrils. He wrapped his arms around her once more and laid his head on top of her hair.

"Let's get out of here," he whispered after a few moments. The crowd of people were still hanging by the fire eager to hear more from Kathy. They snuck away from the crowd and through the camp and into the girls tent. It was empty since everyone was still busy performing or selling their goods.

Heath leaned back against some pillows next to Kathy and picked up his fiddle. He began to play a song she heard him rehearsing earlier. She closed her eyes, letting the night's accomplishment sink in. She felt exhausted while the song Heath was playing was so delicate. She felt a soft breeze enter the tent's entrance, it caressed her cheeks, gently playing with her wavy hair. She wanted this moment to last forever but she knew she would have to leave Heath in the morning. Someone would come in and tell them they were leaving. They'd pack up and head to their new camp. But Kathy would sneak away once they reached a new town. She'd wait for Heath to be asleep before climbing out of the wagon and she'd find her own way to Dublin. At some point the music stopped and she felt the heaviness of Heath's head on her chest.

***

Kathy woke to the sound of birds and the morning light pouring into the tent. She peered around her, they were alone still. She felt disorientated. She had expected to get up in the middle of the night to travel. Kathy cursed under her breath and started to throw the clothes she had laid out earlier in her rucksack. She needed to leave now before Heath woke up. Kathy was about to pull her jacket on when Heath stirred from his sleep and sat up.

"What's going on?" Heath asked, confused.

"I need to leave, Heath," Kathy said, holding her jacket in her arms. "I can't make you go to Dublin with me. You have people here that love you. I'm not going to be the one to take that away from you." Kathy moved to the exit of the tent.

"Kathy wait," Heath jumped up and grabbed her

arm. "You're not doing anything to me. I want to go with you."

"How can you say that when you have Sloane and Cian who care for you so much? And Paddy too who's spent so much time teaching you. How can you leave them all behind for me?"

"Because I love you."

Kathy froze and glanced down at her feet. She felt butterflies in her stomach. Heath grabbed her jacket and threw it on the ground.

"I want to be with you. Why won't you let me in?" he asked, grabbing her shoulders. "I love you. I want to wake up every morning and see you next to me. Sure that means leaving some people behind but that's what it's all about, isn't it? You find someone you love and start a new family."

Kathy's eyes burned with tears. "You don't want me, Heath,"

"Yes I do, Kath. I do."

"I'm broken. You deserve someone whole. I'm not even a Traveller, I'm not anything. I'm just a girl who ran away from an orphanage."

Heath hugged her tight and held her in his arms. "You're so much more than that."

He pulled back to look into her grey eyes. "I want to be with you, please let me."

Kathy stared back into his eyes. She felt a burning in her stomach and against every thought telling her to leave, she leaned in and kissed his lips. She tasted the saltiness of his tongue against her own. Heath pulled the rucksack off her shoulders and threw it across the tent. She felt his tongue against hers and pressed her body against his own. They fell onto the mattress and their breathing deepened and started to match in rhythm. She wanted more from him. She reached for his trousers and unbuckled it. He reached under her dress and slid her pants down her legs. She felt the weight of him on top of her. Felt his hands eagerly pulling up her dress. She held his hips tightly. And when he moved she felt the world shift around her. Rain started to patter against the tent in an eagerness that was matched by their bodies. Kathy gazed up at the Celtic cross that dangled between their bodies. They crumbled into one another, shivering against their cold delights.

***

They laid next to each other breathless. Kathy felt her heart beat inside her chest. Her body felt empty, like all the pleasure was pulled right from her. She reached out to lay against his chest. He held her close and they listened to the rain continue to beat against the canvas tent.

"Something isn't right," Heath said after catching his breath. He was looking up at the ceiling.

"What do you mean?" Kathy asked, rolling onto her side.

"It's daylight, we should have been woken up hours ago to travel through the night."

Heath stood up and pulled his trousers on, he ran his hand through his hair.

"I'll come with you," Kathy said, sitting up and

pulling her pants on. She took her jacket and felt the cold November, morning air wash over her as they exited the tent. They heard voices coming from the centre of the camp. They walked quietly hand in hand and saw everyone standing around Laoise's caravan.

"What is it?" Kathy asked, standing on her tiptoes. The door to her caravan was wide open. Heath walked up and tapped Paddy's shoulder.

"What's going on?" Heath gestured to the caravan. Paddy held his hat between his fingers and shook his head.

"It's Laoise, she took a bad turn after the circus ended. She's been coming in and out of it all night. She only has a few more breaths left," he said, shaking his head. Heath and Kathy pushed through the crowd of people. She was angry. How could they all stand around crying when she wasn't even dead? Kathy climbed up the steps and ran to her bed. Birgitta was in a corner sobbing while Sloane leaned over the old woman, dabbing a cotton cloth against her forehead.

"What's wrong with her?" Kathy demanded, looking helplessly at Sloane. She kneeled and grabbed the old woman's ringed hand. It felt faint and lifeless. Her turquoise spectacles were placed on the side of the bed revealing her papery thin eyelids. Laoise opened them slowly. Her eyes appeared blurry and far away.

"Laoise, can you hear me?" Kathy asked, squeezing the old woman's hand. She turned her head to the side to face Kathy.

"Kathy... I need you to take the chest," she said slowly, each word was a struggle for breath. Kathy shook her head.

"You can't go now, I don't know what I'm doing. I still need you." Kathy sobbed into her hand. She felt a soft squeeze from Laoise's hand.

"Promise me you'll share them. Share the stories."

"Of course I'll share them. But I need you here to help me." Laoise smiled before her eyes closed. Her chest expanded for a final breath before her head gently rolled to the side.

"What did you do?" Kathy yelled at Sloane. "How could you let this just happen?" she demanded. Sloane reached out and gave Kathy a hug.

"There wasn't anything we could do for her. She's been dying for a very long time."

Kathy sobbed into Sloane's shoulder. She felt her body shake with grief. Laoise was the only person in the world who believed in Kathy and now she was gone. Outside the caravan, a long and painful cry came from her black cat.

"C'mon Kath, let's get some air." Heath wrapped his arm around Kathy and held her close as they walked through the crowd of people. Kathy peered back. The cat was circling the front of the caravan, crying loudly. Mary was trying to soothe it with a bowl of milk. Kathy and Heath walked out of the camp and farther into the field.

"She went peacefully, knowing that you'd look after the stories. You helped her with her time."

Kathy hugged her violet, wool dress close to her body.

"How can I keep a promise like that? I don't know

what I'm doing."

Heath pulled her in closer as they gazed toward the horizon. The sun had reached its height.

"She thinks you do or she wouldn't have asked."

Kathy nodded stiffly and wiped her runny nose with her sleeve. "I knew nothing about her... why do I care so much?"

Heath considered this for a moment before he reached his hand out to push a strand of her hair behind her ear.

"Because she knew you my darlin' girl."

Chapter Twelve
The Long Journey to Dublin

They left the next morning for Newry, where Laoise would be buried. They sent word across the country, stopping every tinker and telling every town about her passing. The funeral would take place in a week. Kathy and Heath felt it was important to attend and decided this would be their last trip with the clan. As Kathy sat in the back of the wagon, she imagined what Laoise's caravan was like, being pulled in front of the procession. Before leaving Kells, the Travellers draped black silk across the entire body of the caravan, as if it were her coffin. They pulled it with a black horse.

It was a long journey spent in silence. Kathy felt self-conscious as they moved through the towns. The settlers stared at the long line of caravans and horses that moved their way through the high streets. It was strange to travel in the brightness of daylight. It felt like they were being exposed. The curtain pulled back; no longer hidden by the night.

When they arrived in Newry it was already nightfall. Kathy woke with her head against Heath's shoulder. She could see lights ahead of them and thought they must just be outside of the town. Silently, they climbed out of the wagon and walked around the dewy grass to stretch their legs. She held her coat close to her body and shivered. Even with the wool jumper and her coat she could still feel the wet air chilling her bones.

"What will they do without Laoise?" Kathy whispered, looking over to the group as they pulled their caravans into a spiral, leaving Laoise's caravan outside the circle for the first time.

Heath shrugged. "I don't know, as long as I've been here she's been in charge. I guess it'll be Birgitta."

"Really? But she's so young. Surely it should go to someone older."

"It's not about age, it's about talent. Birgitta's gift outranks anyone else here. Everyone but you, that is," Heath said with a crooked smile.

Kathy shook her head.

"I hope they don't think I'm going to stay," she said nervously, looking around as they unpacked their furniture. Cian lined rocks into a large circle for the fire.

"They might, but I'm sure Birgitta is eager to see you leave."

Kathy laughed bitterly.

***

The next day, Cian and Paddy set out to the funeral home in Newry as the rest of the camp went quietly about their daily chores. Even Courtney couldn't bring herself to critique Bree's chopping technique. Kathy was still expected to receive the first cup of coffee that morning. For a lot of people this break in routine was a nice distraction. It was as if Kathy had naturally moved into Laoise's position. Kathy did her best to avoid everyone. Spending her time walking around the field or down by the river with Heath but whenever they came up for food she would be met with people asking her permission for things.

Even Courtney came up to her that evening, as she and Heath were tucking into a stew, asking rather bitterly if it was okay that she go into town to stock up on some winter reserves.

Kathy awkwardly stuttered, "Yes," while dribbling stew down her chin.

Birgitta became more removed from Kathy. She avoided Kathy throughout the day, spending her time with Braden, Moira and Fallon. Kathy peered over to their group and Birgitta would always meet her gaze with her head held high. Her blue eyes would narrow and Kathy would quickly look away, embarrassed.

On the morning of the funeral, Kathy unpacked her rucksack and lined up the items on her mattress. It was strange to see how different they were from when she first arrived. Her paperback book now shared the bottom of the bag with The Book of Moons she stole from Laoise's caravan all those months ago.

Kathy picked up the red jumper and breathed into the wool. It no longer smelled like Sinead. Instead, it had picked up the smells of its new home; a mixture of dirt and fire. She dug deeper and felt the smooth stone Kira had given her the day before she drowned. Kathy felt a lump in her throat. She missed Kira. Her silence was comforting and steady. She understood Kathy without words. She stroked the engraving before placing the stone into her pocket. She moved her hand to the extra pair of socks Sinead had packed. Kathy could have used these while with the Travellers but she couldn't bring herself to do so. What if she met Sinead along the road and needed the pair herself?

Kathy felt a bulge from the inside of one of the socks and pulled the pair apart. She dug her hand into the wool and pulled out the blue silk scarf that belonged to Birgitta. Kathy thought back to that night. She remembered the way the men pushed Birgitta down and ripped the front of her dress. She remembered the boot marking the silk scarf. It seemed perfectly ordinary now. Only slightly wrinkled from being inside of the sock all these months. She thought it strange how clean and untouched it seemed to her now. Kathy reached down at the lavender dress Mary made for her. She stroked the beads along the neckline and remembered the tiny bracelet Kira made for her.

"Oh..." Kathy heard movement at the front of the tent and turned to find Birgitta at the entrance.

"Birgitta, don't go!" Kathy called, as she watched her turn on her heels.

"What do you want?" Birgitta snapped, crossing her arms. "Don't you have everything? Aren't you special enough now?" She walked closer to Kathy, her eyes narrowed and flaming with rage.

"Heath wasn't enough for you was he? You had to take Laosie too, here take this!" Birgitta pulled at her hair band and threw it at Kathy's feet.

"Take it all. Take my clothes you selfish bitch and maybe that will be enough for you!" she screamed, pulling at her cardigan throwing it at Kathy. She quickly covered her head, avoiding the garment.

"I'm sorry. I didn't mean for this to happen. This isn't what I wanted!" Kathy sobbed back.

Birgitta walked up to her and slapped her across the face.

"Then why did you take it from me," she cried. Kathy dropped to her knees and held her head between her arms. She rocked her body while she sobbed and waited for more. For the kicks or the words. Or anything. She wanted it to come. She glanced up at Birgitta and watched as she brought her closed fists to her mouth and screamed before she pulled at her own hair.

"Why did you come here? It was fine before you came." She dropped to her knees and cried into her hands. She cried into her hands. Kathy reached out to hold her but she pushed back.

"I'm not a Traveller, I never was."

Birgitta sniffed and looked up.

"I don't want any of this. I'm just trying to get to Dublin to find my best friend," Kathy said. "I never meant for any of this to happen. I never meant to be a storyteller. I was just looking to make some money so I could leave without Heath. I'm sorry, Birgitta. I'm so sorry." Kathy buried her face in her hands and waited for her to react. She waited for Birgitta to scream again, for another slap. Instead she felt her arms wrap around Kathy's body and they rocked together. She felt Birgitta's head against her own. She heard her sobs against her own.

"I miss her too," Kathy sobbed. "I'm sorry she's

gone."

Kathy squeezed her shoulders and Birgitta nodded her head as she cried.

"She wasn't supposed to go like this. I'm not ready," Birgitta said, pulling back and shaking.

Kathy wiped her tears on her sleeve. "But you're brilliant. People love you; they'll follow you anywhere."

"What if I get it wrong?"

Kathy reached out to hold Birgitta's hand. "I don't think you can. You were born for this."

Birgitta laughed and wiped her wet face with her hands.

"What will you do?" Birgitta asked quietly.

"Go to Dublin, keep storytelling; it's the least I can do for Laoise." Kathy looked down at her hands.

"Will you take Heath with you?" Kathy nodded.

"He really loves you. I see the way he looks at you. He never looked at me that way." She glanced to the tent entrance, as if expecting him to walk through. "I tried to love him but he was meant for greater things. I'd only hold him back." Birgitta stared at Kathy, her eyes red and puffy, her cheeks blotchy. Despite all this, she was still beautiful.

"We should go," Birgitta said, looking outside. They could hear the horses being attached to the wagons that would bring everyone to the cemetery. Birgitta stood up and walked to where her cardigan lay. She picked it up from the ground, wiping the dirt from it before pulling it over her shoulders. She smoothed the front of her black dress and walked outside.

Kathy threw her things into the rucksack before pulling it on her back and followed Birgitta outside. She reached into her pocket and felt the blue silk scarf. When Kathy entered the camp, she saw Birgitta reaching up for Braden's hand to help her into the wagon.

"Birgitta, wait up!" Kathy called running towards her. Birgitta let go of Braden's hand and turned to face Kathy. Kathy opened her palm to reveal the blue silk.

Birgitta's eyes watered and she gave her a small smile. She reached out her hand and picked the scarf from Kathy's palm.

"Thank you," she croaked.

"I'll see you there," Kathy said, nodding at the wagons.

Birgitta nodded and took Braden's hand again before climbing into the wagon. Kathy waved and turned to find Heath approaching her with Rosie, the white horse, pulling a small wagon behind her. Kathy wrapped her arms around him and tasted his sweet lips against her own.

"It took me some time but I finally convinced them that the storytelling books belong to you," he said, gesturing to the chest neatly packed next to some blankets and Heath's fiddle. Kathy smiled and hugged him closer.

***

Kathy had never seen so many Irish Travellers in one place. Hundreds of people turned up to the small cemetery in Newry to pay their respects.

The procession was long and painful. The casket that carried Laoise's frail body was pulled by black horses. People wept, some fell to their knees. Everyone felt the pain of her absence. When the funeral ended the Travellers moved to the field nearby, pulling Laoise's caravan with them, where they continued their stories about Laoise over whiskey and cigars.

Kathy and Heath walked over to the hole in the ground that held her coffin. It was perverse; too perfectly shaped for a life so complex. Birgitta and Braden stood on the other side, his hand on her waist as she whispered a prayer. She held a small rectangular package wrapped in her blue silk scarf that looked like the shape of Laoise's tarot cards. Birgitta nodded before turning and walking away, her hand firmly grasped around Braden's. They walked past the sycamore tree, up to Mary. She had a black shawl draped over her thin shoulders and she rocked the black cat in her arms. Mary's green eyes met Kathy's as she smiled before turning to follow Braden and Birgitta into the field. In the distance, the smell of gasoline and smoke was wafting in the wind.

Kathy peered into Laoise's grave but she couldn't see her coffin. It was covered with lilies and lilacs. She felt Heath's arm wrap around her shoulder as he pulled her in close. She could feel his heartbeat. Kathy clutched the small leather-bound book to her stomach.

It felt right to share one last story with Laoise. Kathy's hand shook as she opened the book and in a croaked whisper she told her the story of Tír na nÓg. The only story in all her books that had just one version. Heath bowed his head and listened to Kathy's words. When she finished, he glanced up at the headstone.

"I never knew her full name," Heath said sadly, shaking his head. Kathy read the fresh marks in the stone - Laoise Margaret Sheridan. Relief and regret washed over Kathy as she read this name over again and repeated the words in her head. Knowing Laoise's full name made her so much more tangible in Kathy's mind. And yet, it made her more distant. How those three stories of Laoise, Margeret and Sheridan were now lost forever.

Kathy looked up at the neighbouring grave and saw the same old man Kathy and Heath met all those months before. His hair was greyer. He stood leaning against his walking stick with a pipe dangling from the side of his mouth. He glanced up at them as Kathy and Heath walked over. He gave them a quick nod. Heath reached out and with a firm grasp shook his hand.

"Francis Cleary," he replied after Heath introduced himself and Kathy.

"We saw you in our camp back at Templemaley, you were with Johnny," Heath said.

"Ay, we were travelling to Belfast together. The Garda caught up with him in a raid. Poor sod couldn't take another beating," Cleary explained, shaking his head.

Heath brought his hand to his forehead. "That's terrible."

Cleary nodded and inhaled deeply into his pipe. He let out a slow exhale that surrounded them in a cloud of smoke.

"Did you know Laoise well?" Kathy asked, looking over at the open grave again.

Cleary shook his head.

"Not as much as I would have liked. We were good friends long ago but time gave us different roads to travel." He stabbed the walking stick deeper into the soggy grass. "I knew her uncle," he continued, nodding to the grave in front of them. "He and my father were very close," he took another draw from his pipe. "Last of the storytellers they were, them and her mother Margaret." He gestured to the grave next to them. Cleary shook his head and removed the pipe from his mouth.

"Where are you headed now?" he asked, looking at the last few caravans and wagons that were pulling out of the cemetery.

Kathy gazed up to the neighbouring field. A large blazing fire was consuming Laoise's caravan. Its flames swayed in the cold wind.

"Dublin," Heath replied, digging his hands into his pockets.

The man chuckled and placed the pipe on the side of his mouth.

"There's no way yer getting through now." He looked up at the end of the cemetery to the rolling hills in the distance. "Nothing but army trucks are lined along these borders." He shook his head, digging the walking stick into the ground as he leaned against it. "The only way to Dublin is through Belfast," he explained, pulling his jacket closer to his body. "You'll need to take the ferry up to the Isle of Man and switch there to Belfast. It's the safest route for Travellers."

Rain was starting to fall from the grey sky and it was getting colder. Kathy held the leather-bound book closer to her body to protect it from the rain. Cleary's eyes moved to the book she held in her hand. His eyes widened for a brief second, as if he recognised it. Kathy held it against her chest tighter.

"Where did you get that?" he asked, before exhaling some smoke.

"It was a gift, from Laoise."

"Kathy's a storyteller," Heath added proudly, pulling her in close. The man shook his head again and turned from them, walking to an old horse and cart. He walked a few feet before stopping in his tracks and turning around.

"What did you say yer last name was?" he called at Kathy.

"I... I didn't," Kathy stammered. "It's Joyce."

The man barked a cheerful laugh. "There might be hope for us after all!"

He turned around and gave them a short wave before climbing up on the cart, and with both hands on the reins he beckoned his old horse forward.

"Do you think he was telling the truth, about Dublin?" Kathy asked watching his silhouette fade down the lane. She glanced around her; it was just Kathy and Heath in the cemetery now. The rain was picking up and the sun was slowly melting behind them.

"It's only a short ride to Belfast. We could catch a

ferry to the Isle of Man and then to Dublin like Cleary suggested?" Heath suggested.

Kathy shivered and held her arms tightly across her body. She thought of Sinead and wondered if she was somewhere warm. It had been months since Kathy last saw her red curls running down the road away from her. A few more days wouldn't matter, even if it did mean stopping in Belfast to catch the ferry. Kathy and Heath would soon arrive in Dublin and Kathy would find Sinead waiting for her on the stone bridge across the pond in St Stephen's Green.

Kathy looked up and nodded. They walked through the rows of headstones to their horse and wagon. She felt the cold wind touch her brow and listened to the leaves shake. The weight of the engraved stone in Kathy's pocket anchored her as she lifted her hand to the sycamore tree and felt its small leaves brush across her fingers.

When they reached their horse and cart, she pulled herself up onto the wagon. She picked up a plaid blanket from the seat, wrapped it around herself and took some comfort from the small amount of warmth it created on this cold day.

Heath lifted the reins, gently flicked them and urged the horse forward.

Kathy clutched the leather-bound book that was now on her lap. As she looked towards the smoke from the fire she moved her fingers tenderly over the book's title.

For a while they sat in silence, both lost in their respective thoughts.

Heath reached out and squeezed her hand.

"My mother named me after her favourite character in a book," Kathy explained softly, smiling while she gazed toward the horizon. Together they started on the long journey to Dublin, and in that space between light and dark, Kathy told Heath her story.

THE END

Acknowledgements

When I started this novel in 2015, I couldn't have imagined all the places it would take me. In hindsight, it makes sense that I would be so fascinated with a transient people like the Irish Travellers during this period of my life. The idea of belonging somewhere, not to a place, but to a way of life stuck with me. It made me wonder what it would feel like to lose the part of our identity that is defined by place. What stories would tie people together in lieu of this? What happens when these stories start to disappear?

This book is by no means an accurate representation of Irish Travellers, and is meant purely as a work of fiction. However, I sourced as much research material as I could find to depict a realistic picture of this way of life. Janine Wiedel's photographs and transcripts in *Irish Tinkers* helped me imagine what Irish Travellers looked like and sounded like in the 1970s. For insight on what it might feel like to live on the road, I referred to Jess Smith's *The Way of the Wanderers*. For inspiration on the storytelling culture in Traveller communities, I used Duncan Williamson's *Fireside Tales of the Traveller Children*.

I am grateful for the many visits I made to Ireland while writing this book. I am indebted to all the strangers I've met on those winding roads; their words and perspectives have helped shape this story.

Thank you to all my writing friends who have encouraged me to finish this book. In particular, the talented poet and writer, Sussi Louise Smith for her incredible support and words of encouragement, especially when my imposter syndrome kicked in.

Thank you to my good friends Jezemin, Jonathan, Elle, Taylor, Jen and Matthew for cheering me on. To my childhood friends, Josée and Janelle, thank you for being my very first readers and fans.

Thank you to Rick Armstrong and his team at Fisher King Publishing for giving Kathy's story a home, this is truly a dream come true.

Most of all, thank you to my patient and compassionate fiancé, Nicholas, for seeing this through to the very end with me.

Lightning Source UK Ltd.
Milton Keynes UK
UKHW010750030620
364295UK00001B/57